WHAT WE KEEP

HEARTFIRE FALLS

J.H. CROIX

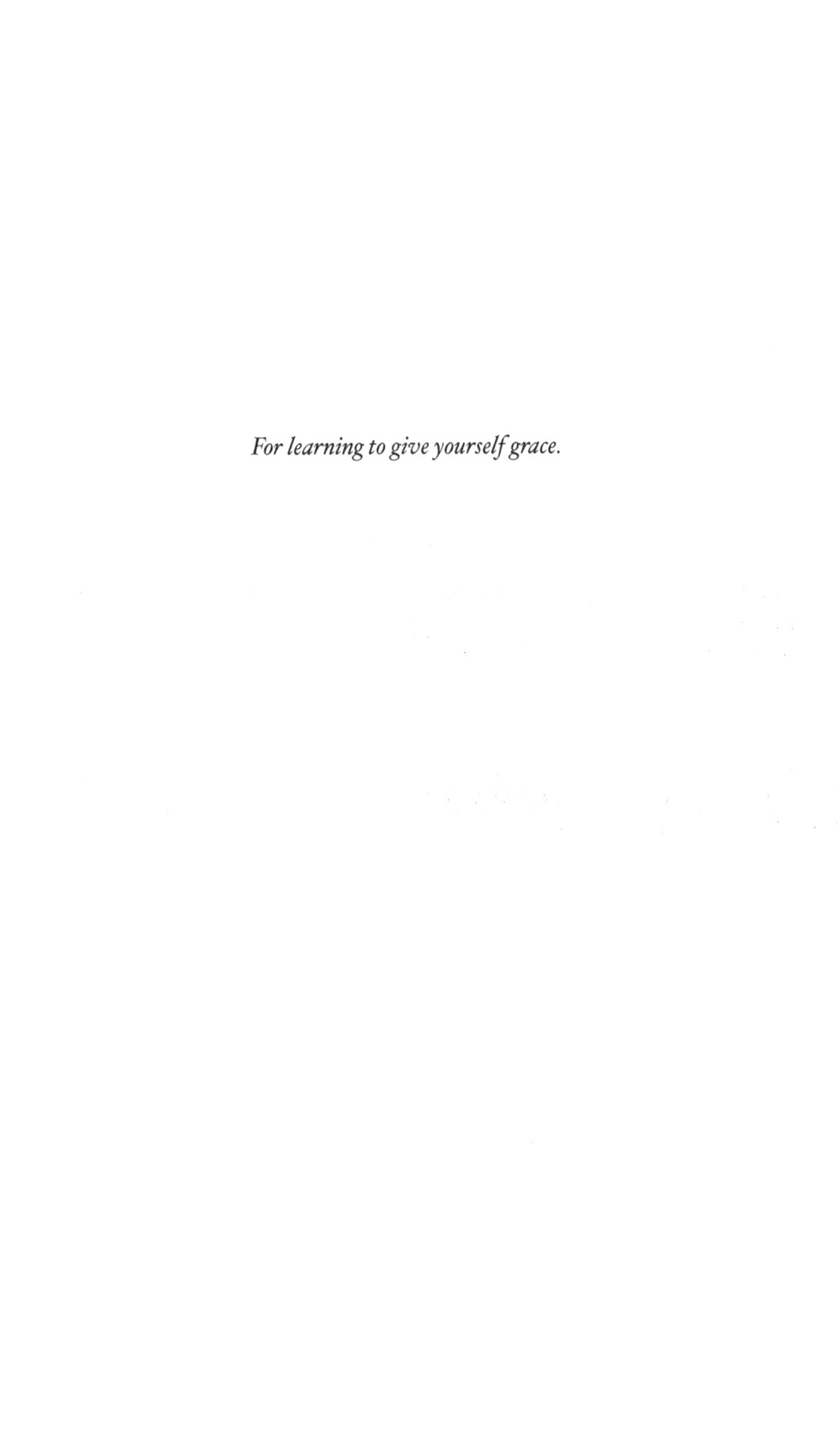

For learning to give yourself grace.

Chapter One

ELSA WHITNEY

The wind whipped through the trees, and I breathed in the crisp air, carrying hints of evergreen and the ocean. I needed this. The rustle of the wind and the trees was just enough to mask the sound of the—

"Oh, my God!" I squeaked.

A goat was running straight for me. "What is happening?" A startled laugh slipped out as I looked on in amazement when two more goats appeared, followed by two more.

The ragtag herd of goats trotted toward me. Something about them was oddly endearing, minus the fact that I was alone, or at least I thought I was, in the wilderness of Alaska.

Okay, maybe not entirely wilderness. I was about twenty miles from the outskirts of a town. Suburbia, I suppose, by Alaskan standards.

Seeing as the goats were aiming straight for me, I didn't know if they were friend or foe. Of all the things I worried about in my life, being trampled by five goats had literally never been on that list. I was a gold-level medal worrier. Life had handed worry to me on a platter when I was a little girl, and no matter how hard I tried to convince my brain otherwise, I knew there were plenty of reasons to worry.

"Just not about goats," I whispered to myself.

I glanced around. Once upon a time, a house had been here. All that was left were the crumbled hints of an old foundation and a few charred beams left behind from the wildfire that had blazed through here a while back. I had nowhere to hide from the goats except maybe behind a tree or my car, which was a good quarter of a mile away. The once-upon-a-time driveway that led here was too deeply rutted, so I'd stopped halfway down.

Deciding to brave the goats, I turned to face them, and they stopped nearby. One of them, bolder than the others, approached me curiously. "Please be friendly," I pleaded.

I'd stared down a few moose in my life in this area, but no moose were around at the moment. All things considered, that might be for the best.

"Hey!" a voice called. The voice appeared to be coming from the direction the goats had come from.

"Maybe you guys belong to someone," I said, looking at the goats.

One of them stretched its nose out toward me. A quick glance confirmed she was a female. She nudged my hand before glancing back toward the voice calling.

"Pinky!" Just then, a little boy appeared. Maybe I wasn't great at guessing children's ages, but I'd put him between eight and ten. He was on the tall side with a bright purple mohawk, glowing like a beacon against the blue sky.

The goat, who had just sniffed me, watched the little boy curiously as he approached, while another goat spun around and trotted in a rapid circle around me. I lifted a hand to wave at the boy just as the trotting goat headbutted me. I let out a startled sound, turning reflexively and promptly falling. The boy's voice reached me, calling for the goats as I heard feet pounding hard and fast on the ground.

The goats stared at me from above a moment later, and the little boy reached us. "I'm so sorry!"

"It's okay," I said. It *was* okay, although my butt hurt.

I looked over at the goat who had knocked me down. This one was almost silver in color, with fluffy hair. My breath puffed in the cool air.

"I guess I wasn't expecting goats," I announced as I looked at the little boy. His blue eyes were serious, a stark contrast to his hair.

"I'm really sorry. They escaped," he explained.

"From where?" I couldn't help but ask as I clambered to my feet.

"Who are you?" the boy asked, ignoring my question.

Before I could answer, another voice called, "Tommy!"

The boy, presumably Tommy, glanced over his shoulder. "Over here, Dad!"

I lifted a hand to shade my eyes. A man approached with long, easy strides, and a sense of familiarity pinged. I thought I recognized him. After all, I *had* grown up here.

"That's my dad," the boy said before belatedly answering my question. "There's a large animal rescue next door. And, well... we have goats now."

Questions tumbled through my thoughts. I didn't know why I was surprised that there was an animal rescue and goats. I hadn't been here in almost fifteen years, to be precise. But when you grew up in Alaska, you tended to feel like the place would stay yours. While I knew there'd be changes, my memory had frozen this place in time. Although that memory included a house long since gone from a wildfire.

"Who are you?" he repeated just as his father reached us.

When the man stepped out of the sun's glare, a bolt of lightning might as well have struck me. He towered over me. I sarcastically considered that he took the phrase tall, dark, and handsome *way* too seriously. He had almost black hair and blue eyes. His striking features were handsome. A bold nose with a little crooked spot in it. Cheekbones so cut I could sharpen a knife on them. Those cheekbones were paired with a cleanly edged jaw and a square chin. His brows were dark slashes. His eyes swept over me just as he repeated the boy's question. "Who are you?"

I started to feel a little defensive. I could've taken the moment to remind this man he knew me, but it rankled that he didn't recognize me. Once I got a good look, that ping of familiarity was confirmed.

"Hey, I own this property, and your goats just walked onto it. And one of them knocked me over!" I put my hands on my hips. "I'm Elsa. Elsa Whitney. You *should* remember me."

Chapter Two

HAVEN SILVER

The woman in front of me, Elsa Whitney, rested her hands on her hips and narrowed her eyes. A gust of wind blew her blond ponytail in a little swirl, and her green eyes shot sparks as she stared at me.

Taking a breath, I gathered myself because when confronted with my high school crush's fiery beauty and the dusting of freckles on her cheeks, my heart pounded hard and fast against my ribs. I hadn't seen Elsa in years. When I'd approached, I thought for sure it was her, but I played it cool. An unexpected sizzle of heat bolted through me. I needed a minute. I'd convinced myself I was well over that old crush, but now she was here, bracingly alive in front of me.

"Elsa, of course," I finally said. "What are you doing here?"

She dropped her hands from her hips and swung one arm in an arc toward the old remnants of a foundation. "Moving home."

Tommy looked over at the old foundation. "There? There hasn't been anybody here since forever," he said.

Elsa's gaze snapped to Tommy. "I grew up here. Before you were born. I might not know how old you are, but I can do math."

"What happened to your house?" Tommy asked. He was never one to hesitate. I'd learned parenting involved accepting my fate—that the questions literally never ended.

Elsa's gaze shifted again toward the traces of what had once been a house. When she brought her eyes back to Tommy, my heart twisted a little at the sadness flickering there.

"It burned down," she said simply.

Tommy opened his mouth to ask another question, but I put my hand on his shoulder. He looked up at me. "What?"

"How about you get Pinky?" Tommy loved Pinky, and at the moment, Pinky was at a distance, eyeing us. She was smart, probably as smart as all of us, and I knew she was calculating just how long it would take Tommy to round her up.

"Okay!" He started running toward her before glancing back. "Nice to meet you, Elsa!"

Her lips curled at the corners, her smile almost seeming like a surprise to her. "Nice to meet you, too!"

The wind blew her hair again, pushing a lock over her eyes. She sent a puff of breath up, expertly dislodging it from the corner of her glasses.

Maybe I hadn't seen Elsa Whitney in about fifteen years, but I could see traces of the girl she had been. Same bright hair. Same pretty green eyes. I hadn't been the only guy with a crush on her in high school. I'd been two years ahead of her when she left town.

One day, she was in the hallways at school. The next day, she was at our place with her mother for a few days. And now, she stood before me. I could feel wisps of grief drifting from her, but more than that was the force of an edge of defiance. Her eyes flashed.

"Tommy's kind of nosy," I said, a chuckle rumbling in my throat.

Her soft laugh was warm, and the sound slipped through me. "Kids are usually curious. But I appreciate that you call it nosy," she replied.

This time, my laugh came out in a bark. "He's ten. If you ever need to distract him, just bring up his goats. He loves them very much."

She shaded her eyes with her hand, looking out toward Tommy, who had rounded up Pinky and the other goats. I could see him talking to Pinky, his favorite, as they walked. I gestured toward the largest of the goats.

"I probably shouldn't, but I let him bring her inside sometimes. She's house-trained."

Elsa dropped her hand and turned to look at me, her eyes brightening as her lips twitched at the corners again. All I wanted to do was make her smile again. And again. And again. "The goat is housetrained?"

My smile was sheepish as I nodded. Tommy disappeared over the small rise, taking the shorter route back to where we lived on the adjacent property.

"I'm sorry you got knocked off your feet," I added.

Elsa lifted one shoulder in a small shrug. "I appreciate the distraction. It was kind of welcome."

I abruptly realized this might be the first time she had come back to this property since she left. I sure as hell knew she hadn't been around town.

"Might as well make it official, but I'm still Haven Silver." I gestured over the rise. "Heartfire Falls, if you recall."

Elsa's sharp green eyes studied me, and I wondered what she knew. While I knew her family's loss, mine was a little messier, and most of it had unraveled after she left town. "Of course I remember you, Haven. We grew up next door to each other."

The funny part of all this was that even though I *had* known Elsa and we'd grown up on adjacent properties, she had no clue I'd had a crush on her back in the day. Alaska made it easy to keep your distance from neighbors and accepted distance in a way that maybe other places wouldn't, even in curious, gossipy small towns.

"I'm moving back home," she said again.

We both turned to look together at the old foundation. "Here?" I asked, gesturing in an arc toward the spot.

She rolled her eyes when our gazes met again. "Not specifically there. I'm not sure what my plan will be, but I'll definitely figure it out."

"I'm sure you will."

Before I knew what was better for me or even thought this through, I offered, "We have room at the resort. You can stay there if you'd like."

Her gaze bounced up to mine again. "Oh, wait. Are you rebuilding Heartfire Falls?"

Chapter Three

ELSA

"Haven Silver," I said aloud in my car.

I knew Haven even though we hadn't really spent much time together. We'd grown up on the outskirts of the small town of Willow Brook, Alaska, and technically lived next door to each other. Although the concept of *next door* in Alaska was a little more stretched out than in most places.

The Silver family owned Heartfire Falls Resort, a wilderness and adventure-type place. I'd always been so curious about them. While my family had consisted of my parents and me, the Silver family seemed huge in comparison. Seven siblings: one daughter and six brothers. Although I wouldn't say we were close, they'd always been nice. All of them.

For years, I'd stayed away from this town until I finally stared down the reality that the only way to banish my ghosts was to storm them. Grief never went away, but sometimes running from it twisted it tighter in your heart.

I glanced in my rearview mirror, taking a glimpse of Haven as I drove away. Even in the *objects in mirror may be closer than they appear* sort of way, his shoulders were broad against the backdrop of the bright blue sky.

"He's married," I murmured to myself in the car as I looked ahead again. I didn't need to think about Haven Silver being handsome. He had a son who he might as well have chewed up and spit out, they looked so similar.

My car bounced a little over the gravel. Maybe this whole thing of coming home was ridiculous. All that was left of my childhood home were remnants of a foundation.

I remembered reading about the Heartfire Falls Resort burning down in the same fire. Logically, that made sense. Ever since the spruce bark beetle kill claimed swaths of Alaskan forest, fires have kept sweeping through areas. While wildfires were part of life here, clusters of dead, dry trees meant the flames had plenty of fuel. Even then, I'd been shocked when I heard about the wilderness lodge burning up. It had happened maybe five years after we left. I'd assumed it would be rebuilt quickly, but that hadn't happened. I guess, until now.

Even though my memories of Willow Brook were tangled with loss, I'd always loved the landscape and could never banish my longing for it. The land itself was stitched into my heart.

At the time, I'd needed the change of location when my mom and I moved away. Years later, I still found myself looking up the news in town because I missed it so much. I wondered how far along Haven was in rebuilding the resort and what it would be like. I also wondered about renting a room there. It could be perfect for me.

As it was, Janet—my mom's old friend, and I suppose everyone's friend in town—had told me she wished she had a space for me to rent, but she didn't have anything available. While I had a few friends from my days growing up here, I didn't have many. We'd lived far enough out of town, and though loving, my father had been offbeat in ways that didn't invite too many people into our world.

I drove into town, pondering how much I'd missed the area along every mile. For tonight, I was staying at Wildlands Lodge. You'd think my car would be packed to the gills, but all I had was one bag and a tiny crate of clothing, just enough to be ready for winter when it came in a few months.

After checking into my room, I made my way down to the restaurant. It was kind of funny that even though this resort was practically a centerpiece of Willow Brook, I'd only been inside a few times. It had always been a place I was curious about, like so many places.

My dad only ever took us to the grocery store on occasion, the pharmacy, gear stores, and school for me. The rooms here were nice, with big beds piled high with pillows and lots of windows offering beautiful views from all angles. Plush carpets in the hallways softened footfalls. The whole Alaska lodge vibe was strong downstairs, with wide, exposed wooden beams crisscrossing the tall ceilings and polished hardwood floors.

I could hear the murmur of voices spilling down the hallway from the restaurant, and anxiety started to spin inside me. I figured I'd always be a little anxious about social situations. Though I'd loved my dad and missed him a whole lot, his quirks meant "living off the land" was a pretty concrete experience.

The woman at the reception desk smiled at me as I walked by. I slipped past the lobby and into the restaurant, looking around and wondering if I should go to the bar or take a table. I didn't want to sit at the bar, because then I might be expected to order a drink. It wasn't that I *didn't* drink, it was just that I rarely did.

The host was a tall, lanky man with a bright smile and twinkling eyes. "Hello, hello," he said. "Where would you like to sit?"

I cleared my throat. "By the windows?"

"You've got it." As we crossed the restaurant, he asked, "What brings you to Willow Brook?"

I cleared my throat again. "I grew up here. But it's been a minute since I was here."

His brows arched, and I saw the questions swirling in his eyes. "So I'm sure you've been to Wildlands?"

"Actually, I haven't. Well, I did *technically* grow up in Willow Brook, but it was a ways out of town. I moved away when I was a sophomore in high school."

"Ah, I see." With a smile, he seated me at the only table left by the windows, which had a beautiful view of the lake.

With autumn nipping at the heels of summer, the days were getting shorter, but they were still long by most standards. The colors of the sunset shimmered on the water, the sky stained with tangerine, gold, and pink.

"A server will be with you in just a few minutes."

After I ordered, keeping it simple with a glass of water and a salmon burger, I glanced around curiously. I kept wondering if I would see anyone I knew. Although I didn't have a lot of friends, I knew people because I had gone to school here.

The little girl in me, a quiet voice always, wanted to have friends in a way I hadn't when I lived here. I forced myself to stop looking around and just enjoy the view. A flock of trumpeter swans drifted across the lake, beautiful in the glow of the setting sun.

Maybe I missed Alaska because the landscape had always been a source of peace for me. I pondered Haven's offer to stay at Heartfire Falls.

After my question, Haven had gone on to explain that, yes, they were rebuilding, and it was due to open soon. I wondered how much he knew about how my dad passed.

His mom had been the one to call the ambulance. My mom had always told me to call Maggie for help if I needed it, so that's what I'd done that day. She'd already called for the ambulance before she got to our house. That help had come too late for my foolish father. I'd always wanted to thank her.

"Elsa?" My eyes lifted to see a familiar woman standing there. My brain rifled through my memories.

"Um, Holly?" I prompted.

Her face broke into a smile. "Yes! What are you doing here?"

"Well," I said slowly, "I'm moving back."

"That's awesome!"

Holly was memorable. We hadn't been too close, but she had always been nice to me. Before I knew it, she was pulling me into a hug. Holly had sat with me that night at the hospital while we waited for news on my father. Even though he had no pulse, they emergency team had still brought him here while they tried to resuscitate him. Holly's hugs were wonderful. "I'm so glad you're here," she said when she stepped back, squeezing my shoulders.

Her eyes were bright, and her blond hair was pulled up in a pony-tail. She was dressed practically, in nurse scrubs.

"Did you become a nurse?" I asked, recalling that she had been at the hospital that night because she was a volunteer then.

She nodded quickly. "Sure did."

Her gaze sobered. "How are you?"

"I'm pretty good," I said. Because I was.

It was hard to explain to anyone, even myself, that even though I'd lost my dad and my childhood had been a little strange because of him, I really was doing okay these days.

"We need to exchange numbers," she said quickly.

Just then, another person I recognized, although I didn't know if he recognized me, approached. Nate Fox.

Holly had been a few years ahead of me in high school, and so had Nate. Living in the small world of Alaska was weird. I'd always felt a little outside of everything, but I knew all the details about everybody. In those days, Nate had been Holly's twin brother's best friend.

When he stopped beside Holly and curled his arm around her shoulders, I quickly realized maybe they were together.

She glanced toward me, her brows waggling. "I hated Nate in high school, but we ended up getting married. Who knew?"

Nate flashed a sly grin. "I knew."

"You did not." She nudged him with her elbow. "You remember Elsa, right?"

"I do, I do," Nate said, his smile warm when his gaze met mine.

I felt nervous all over again and swallowed. "Nice to see you, Nate."

"Good to see you, Elsa. Let me guess, you're moving back? Willow Brook's awesome. Smart move."

Before I could say anything in return, someone called Nate's name. He glanced over his shoulder before bringing his attention back to me. "Welcome home. I'm one hundred percent sure I'm gonna see you again, but I gotta roll."

Holly shook her head slightly, her smile bemused as she watched him walk toward a group of men.

"Nate's a pilot," she explained. "Those are a bunch of firefighters that he flies around. Anyway, give me your number."

I quickly recited it, and she tapped it into her phone. In a few seconds, my phone vibrated with a text.

It's Holly! Put me in your contacts!

"If you need anything at all, just text me," she said. Her gaze sobered. "I'm serious."

Suddenly, I felt choked up. The emotion and weight of returning home were starting to hit me. "I will."

As much as I wanted friends and to connect with the life I had always envisioned having here, instantly getting a hug and exchanging numbers wasn't what I'd expected.

A little while later, I was back in my room, flipping through the channels on the television and smiling to myself. I had, I guess, *sort of* a friend.

Day one was working out okay. I just had to figure out the rest of my life.

Chapter Four

HAVEN

"Cole!" I called as I stepped through the doorway into the main resort.

With my hands full, I lightly kicked the door shut with my boot. "Up here!" my brother called in return.

The sound of footsteps running echoed. "Hey, Dad!" Tommy said as he skidded into the kitchen.

My son's hair stuck straight up, his purple mohawk mussed. He reached for the grocery bags looped in my hands, scooping them up and setting them on the counter. He immediately began digging through them. "Did you get the granola bars?"

"Of course," I replied, reaching over to ruffle his hair.

He found the box of granola bars and tore one open while I began putting the groceries away.

"What's Cole doing?" I asked.

"Finishing some work in the bathrooms upstairs."

I paused, looking around the kitchen. Sometimes it was hard to believe how much work we had done. We hadn't done it all ourselves. It was too big of a job for me and my five brothers. We weren't even all here yet. After the fire, we'd scattered like tumbleweeds in the wind for a little while.

So far, it was Cole, Jude, Grady, and me. Asher had plans to return within the next month. Lincoln was vague as all hell, but I hoped he'd be back sometime. For now, he was traveling all over, fighting fires wherever needed.

Our family's resort, Heartfire Falls, had once been... well, something else. We were Alaska's version of wilderness guides, doing everything from hiking, fishing, hunting, backcountry skiing, and mountain climbing with visitors. It had all fallen apart—literally burned to the ground—when a wildfire blasted through the area so fast it couldn't be contained just over eleven years ago.

My eyes landed on Tommy. He was the marker of *before* and *after.* Our only sister, Bree, had almost died in the fire and eventually succumbed to the infection from her severe burns. Tommy was her son. Tommy's father had skipped town once he found out she was pregnant. When we had an attorney track him down after she passed away, he didn't even hesitate to sign away his rights. To this day, that smarted a little for me because Tommy was a gem of a kid. But then, his loss was our gain. As the oldest, I adopted him. I'd never even contemplated any other option. Our father had passed away a few years before the fire from a heart attack. The losses felt painfully close and compounded each other.

Out of those ashes of that fire came Tommy, and the rest of us were trying to come together to rebuild what we lost.

"Where's your grandma?" I asked, mentally kicking my thoughts back to the present.

Tommy glanced up after he finished the last bite of his granola bar. He inhaled food faster than he breathed. "In the garden."

With the insurance money after the fire, we scrambled to repair the old barn on the property and lived in the upstairs. It was crowded, but it was home. We took the rest of the money and planned carefully as all hell to gradually rebuild the entire resort over the past few years. It was a massive project, but we were almost done.

I wanted it to be better than it had been. We all did. Except maybe Lincoln, but he was complicated. Then again, we were *all* complicated.

The situation had been what most would call a tragedy. I hated thinking about it like that and tried to downplay it in my mind. I gave myself another mental shake. This was high on the list of things I didn't need to dwell on.

Tommy helped me finish putting the groceries away before he started to bolt out of the kitchen again.

"Homework status?" I called after him.

He stopped at the doorway, practically vibrating in place. He had so much energy, and he was constantly on the move. "Done."

I grinned. "Excellent."

"I'll go check on the goats."

"Figured that's where you were headed," I teased lightly. "Good call."

After the fire, my mom started renting out another barn and part of the property to a nearby animal rescue. Their main building, closer to town, was where they took in regular rescues—cats, dogs, and small animals—but they needed space for the larger animals. With over five hundred acres to call our own, we had more than enough of that.

Tommy loved helping with the rescue, and they paid him. I watched through the window as he ran across the yard toward the rescue barn in the distance, carefully closing the gate to the pasture area behind him.

This afternoon was chilly even though it was late summer. The crisp autumn air would chase away summer soon enough. Out in the garden, I spotted my mom trimming her beloved flowers. Turning away from the window, I cut through the kitchen, down the hallway, and pushed through the door connected to the main resort.

We had much of this section finished, so it wouldn't be long before we could have guests. Jogging up the stairs, I found Cole adjusting a light fixture above one of the bathroom sinks in a guest room.

I glanced around. "Looking good."

He finished tightening a screw and flashed a grin. "All done."

"With this one?"

"All of them in this section. We can officially have the code guy come out."

I approached, lifting a hand for a high five. He slapped his palm against mine. "Nice, man. Thank you."

"We just have, you know, ten more rooms to take care of," he replied with a wry grin.

I threw my head back with a laugh. "You know what? It's a fucking miracle we're almost there."

"Damn straight," Cole agreed.

He ran a hand through his dark hair, his eyes crinkling at the corners when his gaze met mine again. "What's for dinner?"

I shrugged. "I picked up some groceries for the week. We could always think about ordering takeout, but we'd have to go get it." We were far enough out of town that delivery wasn't an option. "But I did get a roast chicken. And we've got plenty of frozen pizza," I added.

"Let's make frozen pizza. It's the easiest thing."

We walked together down the hallway, and I glanced around, a smile tugging at my lips. We really were almost there.

———

A few hours later, I leaned back in my chair, balling up my napkin and tossing it in the trash can.

"Nice shot," Jude said with a grin.

Tommy glanced between Jude and me, his eyes twinkling. "Play for five?"

My mom laughed softly. "You'll do anything for five bucks," she teased him.

Tommy tipped his head to the side. "Honestly? I'd do it for free."

She ruffled his hair. "You're a good egg."

"Speaking of eggs," Tommy offered, "the chickens are going crazy. We had a dozen eggs today."

"Did we now? I'll make omelets for breakfast," my mom said.

Maggie Silver was the heart of Heartfire Falls, even if it was just now returning to its glory. I didn't like to contemplate it too much, but the version of her for a few years after our dad passed, and the fire, had been faded, like those old photos where you couldn't quite see what it might have been like in full color. She'd lost her spark for a while, and it pained me.

This resort was her heritage. Her grandparents had been the first to come to Alaska. They'd built something small, which her parents then turned into more and made it an official business. She and my dad kept it going. Between losing our dad and then Bree, the fire had burned away so much.

Somehow though, what had sprouted in the aftermath was my mom in her full glory—bright, sarcastic, warm, and bossy as hell. When we'd been trying to figure out what to do about Tommy after Bree died, I'd offered to formally adopt him. There was *never* any question we would keep him, but she was worried she was too old. We were all his family, and that would never change.

"You boys play napkin basketball. I'll clean up," she said, standing from the table.

"Mom, you don't have to—"

She glanced over. "I haven't done a thing in the kitchen all day, Haven. Let me do this." She gestured at the dishes. "It's the extent of taking plates to the dishwasher and putting the pizza boxes in the trash bins." Her eyes twinkled.

Cole, Jude, and Grady started with the trash talk once the napkin basketball began. Tommy was all focus.

"I've got this," he announced after his third basket.

Jude got cocky and tried to do a bounce shot. Meanwhile, I just plain missed.

"You're not gonna believe who I saw today," I said after we paid Tommy his winnings.

Tommy piped up. "Oh, that's right! There's a lady next door."

My mom hung the dish towel on the oven handle, turned to face me, and rested her hands on the counter. "Who?"

"Elsa Whitney," I said.

My mom pressed her palm to her chest. "Elsa?" she breathed, eyes widening.

"Seriously?" Jude asked.

"Yeah. And she said she used to live there. But there's just all that crumbled concrete." Tommy shook his head, puzzled at this.

But then, he wasn't born until after the fire. He had no idea how much had burned up in a single afternoon.

My mom's voice softened. "Elsa Whitney... Good for her. It's her property. I hope she makes something beautiful there. She was always a good girl."

Chapter Five

ELSA

"Take your sweet time," I said to the moose, who couldn't hear me as it crossed the road in front of my car. She stopped to nibble on some alder by the corner. When I honked my horn, she slowly glanced over, giving me an ear flick, before making her way into the parking area of a gas station.

I laughed to myself, a fizzy sense of joy rising inside me. I had forgotten a lot of things, but I'd missed how often the moose were around. They had a deceptively ambling gait, but their legs were so long they could cover ground quickly, even when it looked like they were taking their sweet time.

As I drove down Main Street in Willow Brook, Alaska, much had changed, yet much remained the same. The mountains were ever-present, a towering backdrop against the bright blue sky. Snow-tipped and jagged, they were the steady presence of my childhood, unshakable and beautiful.

There were familiar storefronts and new ones, but the town still had the same feel with brightly colored signs, a mix of people walking down the street, and tourists standing out with their shiny gear. Although autumn was approaching, there were still RVs galore, slowing traffic.

Willow Brook was the closest town to where I grew up, but I'd mostly only come for school and the occasional errands with my mother. The town had one grocery store, one pharmacy, and one sort-of mini department store. Before moving to come home, I'd done a little research to see if Willow Brook had grown. Its proximity to Anchorage—forty-five minutes to an hour, give or take, and depending on the weather—meant that many large businesses were in Anchorage. Willow Brook was lucky enough to get the tourist overflow. The people who wanted the small-town Alaska experience could get it without going too far out of their way.

Large swaths of Alaska were entirely off the road system and only reachable by boat or plane. Any of the towns on the road system got a lot more visitors.

I knew exactly where I wanted to go, and my lips curled into a smile as I turned into the parking lot for Firehouse Café. After we moved away, Janet James never stopped reaching out. This was her café and, in a way, the town's heartbeat.

I parked, feeling a sting of tears in my eyes as I gathered myself to walk in. Janet and I had emailed and texted, but the café had been closed when I drove into town. She'd told me Luna Talton was taking it over sometime in the next few years. I didn't know much about Luna, although I knew she'd moved away when her parents became RV influencers.

Honestly, when I thought about my time here in Willow Brook, I knew a lot of people's names—like Holly's—and I knew them in passing. But I had never been allowed to go to slumber parties or bring kids out to our house. So I felt like I had snapshots, like looking at somebody's high school yearbook, except I had lived here.

"You're not living that life anymore," I told myself in the car.

I took a breath, climbed out, and crossed the parking lot, pausing to glance up at the bright red sign with the outline of a fire truck. A cheery bell jingled above the door when I walked in. The café was crowded, the air rich with the scent of sweet and savory foods mingling with coffee. The welcoming space had brightly colored art on the walls, fireweed flowers painted on the old fire pole in the center of the space, tables scattered around, and the low murmur of customers in conversation.

When my mom and I would stop in when I was growing up, Janet was never too busy to chat with us and always made me feel like I belonged. As my gaze arced around, I recognized Luna. The woman at the counter with her wasn't familiar. When I heard Janet call her Casey, I mentally clocked that I didn't recall a Casey from childhood.

A moment later, I was waiting at the counter, and Janet was counting out the change someone had handed her. When her eyes lifted to mine, her face cracked into a wide smile. "Elsa!"

I cleared my throat. "Hi, Janet."

That was all I said, and considering the intensity of emotion rising inside me, it felt inadequate. Janet had meant so much to me when I was younger and always would. She had been a bright spot in an otherwise sort of odd life for a little girl.

When it all came to a screeching halt, she comforted me amid a startling loss. To this day, sometimes I wished we'd stayed here, but I needed the space and the change of scenery at the time. Growing up, I never had internet or a cell phone, so I'd never developed the habit of zipping messages back and forth the way so many people did.

When my father died unexpectedly, the loss had been a shock. He'd been one of those off-the-grid, prepper types. He was kind and loving, if a bit flaky. Even when I was little, I'd known my life wasn't like that of most kids. As a result of his choices to keep us pretty isolated, I was still socially reticent.

All these thoughts spun through my mind as Janet rushed around the counter and pulled me into a comforting hug. Her eyes twinkled with her smile when she stepped back and squeezed my shoulders. "Elsa," she repeated. "Come in the back."

"Janet, I know you're working. I don't mean to interrupt your day."

Ignoring me, Janet grabbed my hand and led me around the counter. She stopped beside the woman I didn't recognize. "This is Casey. She works here," she said.

"In case that wasn't obvious," Casey teased, nudging Janet in the side with her elbow.

Janet rolled her eyes. "This is Elsa Whitney. She grew up in Willow Brook, went away, and now she's back."

Casey's gaze was warm. "Nice to meet you. I'm new-ish here."

"I sort of am too," I replied.

A pile of customers came in, and Casey threw me another smile before saying, "Busy, but I'm usually here, maybe not always, but often. I'm sure I'll see you around."

Janet tugged me through the swinging door. "Do you remember Luna?" She gestured toward Luna, who smiled at me.

I felt nervous as I nodded. I didn't know what Luna knew about me. "I think so. I remember you from school."

"Elementary school, and then I moved away. Welcome back!" Luna's wild, dark curls were pulled up into a ponytail.

"Her parents became RV influencers," Janet offered up.

Luna rolled her eyes. "It was fun for about five minutes."

"If you did the online thing, my parents had a whole channel. They made me go by the name Jane online, you know, to protect my privacy. I even straightened my hair, which was a nightmare." Luna rolled her eyes.

A laugh sputtered out of me. "Oh."

Janet paused, looking between Luna and me. I could tell she was considering what to say. "You don't have to explain my life," I said. "You can just... I don't know." I shrugged.

Janet's expression sobered instantly. "Elsa, I mean—"

Luna's gaze had sobered too. I took a deep breath, marshaling my composure. "I'm okay." And I really was okay. I would always miss my dad, but I'd found a way to emotionally climb over the hill of anger about how he got so sick. "I'm okay, Janet," I repeated. "Really. I'd rather just be direct. My dad was a wacky, if loving, guy who got sick and wouldn't go to the hospital. I was with him when he died."

That wasn't the whole of it, but it covered the main points. Luna reached out, taking both of my hands and squeezing gently.

"I know a little bit about what it's like," she said. "Maybe not *that* specifically, but having something big that starts to feel overwhelming. It's life, right? Life is messy and complicated. I'm sorry about your dad."

All of a sudden, my eyes were stinging with tears. Luna, who I hadn't seen since elementary school, pulled me into a hug, and it comforted me more than I could've imagined.

When I stepped back, Janet's eyes were shining with tears. "I'm so glad you're here," she said. "Now, I'm gonna make you something. What do you want? Tea? Coffee?"

"I'll just take your strong house coffee with a bit of cream and toffee syrup."

Janet smiled. "Coming right up. You need to try Luna's donuts. They're amazing."

After Janet bustled out to the front, I looked over at Luna. "Thank you," I said.

"For what?"

"That hug."

She shrugged a little, her curls bouncing as she turned to check a timer on the oven. "I know a little bit about what it's like to feel weird and out of place. Obviously, the details are wildly different." She let out a sigh as she pulled a tray of donuts out of the oven and slid them onto the stainless-steel table running through the center of the room.

She gestured to a stool across from her. "Sit. For years, I didn't even have any friends because being part of the whole influencer world is so weird. I'm so grateful to be here and doing this, and it looks like Janet, as she does for so many of us, is smoothing the way for you."

I nodded. "She is."

"Where are you staying?" Luna asked.

Just then, Janet returned from the front, overhearing Luna's question. "It's driving me crazy that I don't have a place to rent for you," Janet said. "I have been asking all over." She let out a deep sigh. "This whole short-term rental world has really screwed things up. I prefer to do long-term leases, so I just have a short-term rental for tourists, but it's booked up. Ever since they reopened the ski lodge, it's been, well, busy. And I don't even know if you know, but out near you, they're rebuilding Heartfire Falls."

Luna's brows hitched up. "I hadn't heard that. You mean the old wilderness resort?"

"It burned down maybe ballpark ten years ago. Same time that your old house burned." Janet nodded toward me. "Now, they're rebuilding it, which will be good. Willow Brook could use something like that. Speaking of something you could use..." Janet handed me my coffee.

I took a sip and sighed. "Oh, this is so good!" I exclaimed, savoring the rich flavor with a hint of sweetness.

"As soon as Luna's donuts cool, you have to try one. They're amazing." Janet repeated her earlier comment.

Luna chuckled. "Janet, even if they weren't amazing, you would pretend they were."

"But they *are* amazing," Janet insisted, sprinkling sugar over the tray of donuts. "Give it a few minutes so they don't burn your mouth."

"Speaking of Heartfire Falls," I said, "I ran into Haven Silver and his son, Tommy. He mentioned he has a few rooms available. I wanted your opinion."

"My opinion on what?" Janet sat down on a stool beside Luna.

"What's the deal there? Should I take him up on that? My plan is to eventually build out at the property, but that's not going to happen anytime soon."

Chapter Six

ELSA

"Haven Silver is a good man," Janet began. "He and his brothers are working hard to get the resort up and running. It's pretty far along, and I think you should take him up on his offer."

"What's the deal with him?" I asked. "When did he have a son?"

"Haven adopted Tommy. That was Bree's little boy." Janet's expression softened. "She died in the fire, and his father wanted nothing to do with him."

"Tommy was—" Janet's words cut off abruptly when she let out a breath. "Just born."

"Bree died?" I breathed. I hadn't heard that detail. Not that I'd have expected to hear it from one encounter with Haven.

Janet nodded, sadness flickering in her eyes.

Heartfire Falls was beside where my family's home had once been. Despite the isolation of my life with my prepper dad, I knew the Silver family. They'd always seemed like a kind, fun-loving, busy family.

I took a quick breath. "That's so sad. I knew the fire burned down the resort, along with our house, but I didn't know Bree died."

"She was pregnant," Janet added quietly.

I exhaled slowly. "Oh, wow..." My heart ached.

Janet nodded. "She was in the hospital while they tried to save her. The baby survived, but she didn't."

"So Haven adopted him," I said, almost to myself.

"Tommy has all of them, but they scattered a little bit after the fire. Maggie was worried she was too old to formally adopt Tommy. I'm sure it would've been fine, but I understand her point. If something happened to her, they'd be back sorting out next steps all over again. Haven stepped up, but he's that kind of man. Haven has his law degree and worked his tail off to get the insurance claim from the fire approved. He had to go to court and everything. They've been working on it for a few years now," Janet added. "I'd say take him up on that offer. Then you're right there beside your property. It'll give you time."

I squared my shoulders and took a breath. "I need time."

Janet reached for a donut and handed it over. I took a bite, and the sweet, subtle flavor broke across my tongue. "Is that lemon?"

Luna nodded.

"I see why everyone loves these," I said, taking another bite and savoring the sweetness. "It's so good."

"If you need anything," Luna said, "just ask. I'm here all the time."

"It's so good to be back," I admitted, almost a little surprised that was how I felt. Although I'd missed Alaska the whole time I'd been gone, I'd worried maybe my memories of how I felt here wouldn't match up when I was actually here.

———

When I drove out toward Heartfire Falls later that day, my nerves felt strung tight as I followed the winding road leading to the resort. Although we'd lived next door, *next door* in Alaska was almost a half mile away.

Of course, *that* version of the resort had burned down. Heartfire Falls had been known as a world-class fishing and guiding retreat. I remembered my dad grumbling about the tourists, but he'd been friendly with Grant Silver, their father.

Before I'd headed this way, I'd texted Haven since I had his number. His reply had been brief.

Haven: *I'm here. Stop by anytime.*

As I drove along, I passed by a barn, one of the original buildings that survived the fire, judging by how weathered the wood was. Horses grazed in a pasture, their tails flicking, and I couldn't help but laugh when I saw a cluster of goats in a smaller pasture nearby.

When I rounded a curve and the resort came into view, my breath caught. Alaska wasn't short on breathtaking views, but this one *still* surprised me. The resort sat on a rise overlooking the valley stretching beyond it. A glacier glittered in the distance, its icy expanse a stark contrast against the evergreen-covered mountains encircling the area. This rise was so high that I could see the ocean in the distance. At the base of the valley, a wide stream fed from the ocean miles away snaked through, and it was one of the most coveted fishing spots in the area. Salmon would make their way upstream here every year, spilling over the falls that gave the resort its name.

The lodge's exterior looked finished, its wood siding blending into the landscape, while a bright red roof made it pop against the sky. Two small wings stretched from the central building. Everything about it looked solid, and its presence comforted me.

I pulled into a small parking area and cleared my throat as I stepped out. An eagle screeched overhead, and I glanced up just in time to see it soaring over the open field before landing in the trees near the stream. The air smelled crisp and clean with scents of fresh spruce, earth, and something hinting at the nearby glacier-fed water. After walking up the steps, I stopped in front of the door, red to match the roof, and knocked.

My heart pounded in my chest so fast that my breath felt short. I was nervous for a whole bunch of reasons. When no one answered at first, my nerves twisted tighter. Then I heard footsteps, and suddenly, the door swung open.

Haven stood there, his eyes locked with mine. "Elsa," he said simply.

My heart went wild, hammering in my chest and sending heat blasting from my head to my toes. I stared up at him for too many beats.

"Hi," I managed, stumbling over the word. "I was wondering about the rental."

Chapter Seven

HAVEN

The evening before

"Elsa, Elsa, Elsa," Jude teased.

Cole eyed him. "Are you practicing how to say her name?"

I narrowed my eyes. "Jude..." I warned.

"Just wondering if that crush is still a thing," Jude said in a singsong voice.

"Oh, for fuck's sake," I muttered.

Jude shrugged, waggling his brows.

"Dude, don't," I warned. "It's been years. It was high school."

"Yeah, but—" Cole cut in.

"But what?" I prompted. "I've even had a relationship." As if *that* had anything to do with my only high school crush who'd materialized in my world in the here and now.

"What relationship?" Jude interjected.

"I dated..." I had to scramble in my memory. "Sherry, in college."

Cole's brows rose as he cast me a skeptical look. "I don't even know who you're talking about."

"Dude, that wasn't even serious," Jude said with a hard eye roll. "You just went through the motions of dating."

I decided to barrel through this. "Well, Elsa's staying. Mom would want us to let her stay. She doesn't have anywhere to stay because their house also burned in the fire."

"This isn't about her staying," Jude said. "It's about your crush."

"Guys, please don't do this." I didn't need this, not today. Or any day, for that matter.

"Okay, fine. We won't," Cole said. "We'll save it for leverage." He tossed a sly grin over his shoulder.

My brothers left me in peace, and I carried on filling out paperwork. There was *so* much fucking paperwork to deal with, and this part got assigned to me because I was the idiot who went to law school to make money. I did get that degree, but I kind of hated the work. Now I was home, doing what was way better than law school—being a firefighter and getting ready to start wilderness guide trips again. Yet I was still dealing with all the legal papers associated with the insurance and the mess after the fire.

I wished my brothers didn't know that I'd once had a crush on Elsa, but they did, and they didn't hesitate to gleefully remind me now.

She was *that* girl for me back then, but a few years younger than me, so I left her alone. She moved away, and that was that. I let out a sigh.

I hadn't seen her in years, and just because she was still as cute as could be and bright as a drop of sunshine didn't mean I was still crushing on her. Not at all.

———

That evening

"Do you remember how her dad was?" my mom asked.

"A little," I replied, rifling through my memories.

What I remembered about Elsa's dad was a series of fragmented memories that didn't quite make sense. Seventeen-year-old boys weren't known for their discernment. But I did know that things at her family's home had been, well, odd. Her dad had been one of those prepper guys, totally into the off-the-grid life. He'd been loving in a bumbling sort of way.

"He got sick and died, right?" I prompted.

My mom nodded. "That's the easy explanation. He got pneumonia and wouldn't go to the doctor. He didn't believe in modern medicine, vaccines, or anything like that. Lucky for Elsa, her mom made sure she had all her vaccines. Anyway, that fool man had Elsa and her mom trying to keep him alive on their own. Elsa was with him when he died. The poor girl called me because her mom had gone to town to get some medicine, to try to talk him into taking something, anything to help."

"Oh wow. That's awful." I shook my head.

"It was. His folly led to his daughter feeling like she couldn't keep him alive when he should've gone to the hospital the minute he got that sick." My mother clucked. "Elsa was only fifteen. Elsa was just a sweetheart, you know?"

I *did* know. Elsa had always been *that* girl to me once I was old enough to pay attention to girls.

———

Back to this afternoon

Elsa had been just as pretty then as she was now. My adolescent self had been moonstruck over her in high school. Crushes that happened in the midst of the rush of teenage hormones were made of heady stuff. I'd hardly seen her even though she lived next door. These thoughts tumbled through as she stood before me. Her blond hair twirled from a gust of breeze. Sunshine. I always thought of sunshine with her. Her golden locks, those green eyes, and that fresh-cheeked beauty spun together with her smile.

A moment of silence stretched between us. Elsa looked uncertain, as if she wasn't sure what to do next.

"Let me show you around," I finally offered, having no clue how long I stood there staring at her.

She nodded, and I contemplated where to take her. I'd offered her a room to stay, and we had plenty to choose from, but it needed to be a practical choice because we would open soon.

"It looks amazing," Elsa commented, her voice soft.

I glanced down, momentarily drawn into the depths of her gaze. Her eyes were mostly green with shimmering flecks of brown and gold.

"We'll start in the kitchen," I said, leading her forward. "My mom is ecstatic about being able to cook for guests here."

A small smile pulled at her lips. "I bet she is." Elsa spun around. "I don't remember much of how it was before, but this is really nice." She paused, her gaze sobering. "I'm sorry about the fire."

My jaw tightened slightly. "Wildfires happen all the time. You all lost your house too."

"I know, but we weren't here," she said softly.

I couldn't dwell on this because that meant pondering losing Bree. "I'm grateful we can rebuild. The old one was…" I hesitated, choosing my words. "Well, *old*. My great-grandparents originally built it, and then each generation kept adding on. Up through my mom and dad." I shrugged. "And here we are now."

Another silence stretched between us. All of this brought to mind how her dad passed, and I wasn't sure what to think or say or if I should acknowledge it at all.

She looked up at me. I imagined that event had been a dividing line in her life—just as the fire had been a dividing line in ours. There was the *before* and the *after*.

I tipped my head to the side. "How *are* you?"

It might be an out-of-place question at the moment, but somehow, it made sense. An unexpected feeling of kinship flourished between us.

When something or someone truly significant was lost in your life, it was easy to feel alone. As if no one else could grasp how *big* it felt in your small world. Though my details were wildly different from Elsa's, I felt like she understood. Maybe she understood beyond the surface how disruptive the fire had been for my family. Just as I could perhaps understand pieces of what she had gone through.

She was quiet, her gaze softening. "Just like you can't change the fire," she said, "I can't change my father passing away. I've learned to live with it. I came home." Her shoulders rose as she took a slow, deep breath. "Thanks for asking."

I wanted to hold her close. Although it felt okay to acknowledge the ghosts of loss dancing in our lives, I wasn't sure hugging her just now would make sense to her. Even though I deeply wanted to.

"Let me show you around," I repeated, forcing my focus away from Elsa.

I took her through the kitchen first, then back through the open space we had walked through to get here and gestured to the two hallways stretched off the sides.

"We have enough rooms for twenty guests at the moment," I explained. "Jude and Cole have backup plans for up to forty."

"Forty?" Elsa's eyes widened as she stared up at me.

I chuckled. "That's what I said." I shrugged. "Since we got to redo this place from the ground up, if we *can* expand, and if we have enough guests and interest, we figure, why not?"

Elsa's lips curved into a small smile. "Aim high," she said lightly.

"Let me show you the staff rooms," I continued. "We don't have any staff yet. Unless you count Cole, Jude, Grady, my mom, and me."

"What about Tommy?" she asked.

I grinned as we walked. "And Tommy. He helps out with the rescue animals, and he loves it. And they *do* pay him. Rest assured on that."

When she smiled again, my pulse kicked up. The need that had been simmering in the back of my mind since I first laid eyes on her the other day sharpened its claws. Once we reached the main entry, I led her upstairs.

"For now, we have this upper floor above the kitchen and the common area. If we get busy enough, we'll add a second story above the guest rooms."

"Oh, wow." Elsa spun in a little circle, taking it in.

"There's also a finished space on the upper floor of the barn," I added. "I'll take you out there. That's where I stay."

"Tommy seems like he's doing great," Elsa commented as we walked outside.

I flashed her a smile. "He is. He's happy we're rebuilding this place."

"How long has this taken?" she asked as we walked down the stairs.

"We've been working on it for almost three years now. It took years to get all the insurance stuff sorted after the fire. I don't do much with it, but I have a law degree and kept my license. I had to threaten to sue. That's—" I shook my head, almost to myself. "It was a lot of tedious work. We had a crew to help with the foundation and framing, but we've done all the finishing ourselves. Insurance helped, but it only went so far, and we wanted to improve it."

I gestured around. "I don't know how much you know about how Heartfire Falls operated before, but we did guide trips. Fishing, hunting, climbing, ice climbing, hiking, you name it, we did it. We upgraded the smaller buildings first since we needed somewhere to stay."

"Where did you originally stay after the fire?" Elsa asked.

"Upstairs in the barn," I admitted, rolling my eyes as I gestured toward it. "We did some quick work to make the apartment up there work for us."

I led her into the barn. "Come on in." I walked her up to the upper floor, gesturing around. "And this is where I stay."

Her gaze arced about the space. "It's nice."

I shrugged. "We did our best. There are three rooms for you to choose from," I added, leading her down the short hallway. "We've got a few rooms ready in the resort, but between my brothers, my mom and Tommy, there's not much privacy at the moment. Tommy was staying out here with me, but he likes being close to the action in the new building."

She lingered by one of the rooms. "Do you mind if I take this one?"

It was beside mine, but I didn't offer that detail. "I said you could take any."

Peering inside, she lifted her gaze to the windows, which offered a stunning view of the field beyond, currently ablaze with fireweed in bloom, a landscape of fuchsia. "I like this one. What's the rent?"

"Nothing."

Elsa put her hands on her hips. Her eyes flashed. "Haven, you *have* to charge me something."

Chapter Eight

ELSA

"I wasn't going to rent these rooms," Haven said, eyeing me steadily. "They're going to be for staff we eventually hire."

"Well, then give me something to do," I insisted.

"Like what?"

I rolled my eyes. "Something."

He let out a short breath, something close to amusement flickering in his expression. "Let me think about it. You can move in whenever you need to."

"Are you sure?"

"I'm sure."

Haven looked at me expectantly, waiting for me to say something. Something else flickered in the depths of his blue eyes, like the ocean right before a storm when lightning rippled across the sky.

"Are you sure that's okay?" I felt pressed to ask again.

His lips kicked up at one corner, just slightly. "Of course, it's okay."

I shifted on my feet, feeling antsy and nervous. "I need to pay something," I pressed.

Haven's brows hitched up. "I already said that wasn't necessary, Elsa."

"I know, but either let me pay or give me something to do. To earn my keep."

"We need staff more than we need money. Honestly, we've been running ourselves ragged trying to get this place ready to run again."

A long pause settled between us. My thoughts spun to Bree. I was still trying to wrap my brain around the fact that she died. They had seemed like a happy family. Bree had always been nice to me, back when I felt so awkward and out of place in a world my father viewed with deep suspicion.

"I bet it was tough to even get to the point of rebuilding," I said softly.

Haven's sharp features softened. "It was." A beat of silence followed. "It *is*," he added. "We really need to be open, like yesterday or maybe a year ago. But we have to meet code and all that. I knew once we started, it would be hard to finish if we tried to open before we were ready."

"Makes sense."

"What have you been doing for income during all this?" I asked.

"Well, we're all firefighters and pilots. So that's what we've been doing. While I have that law degree, I don't love the work, but here and there, I handle small things." He hesitated for a second, then asked, "Do you remember Nate?"

"Nate Fox," I said. "I ran into him with Holly the other night."

Haven smiled a little. "That's the one."

"He does contract work for the firefighting teams, and we fly the smokejumper planes with him. Sometimes we work the fires ourselves."

"Is that hard after the fire here?" I internally flinched at my own question. That was me, queen of the obvious and awkward questions.

Haven tipped his head to the side, quiet for a few beats. Long enough that I worried I shouldn't have asked. Yet he didn't seem bothered by it. "Fires are getting worse everywhere out West. Summers are hotter and drier. Alaska's no exception." He exhaled, his shoulders stiffening slightly. "Obviously, the fire here was awful, but that's not the hard part if that makes any sense."

It made sense and was something I understood deeply. My father's sad and needless death was painful, but it was separate from me in some ways. Like the fire itself wasn't what hurt Haven, but the loss of his sister.

Strangely, I felt a sense of relief around it. Not relief that others had experienced hardship and loss—never that—but relief in knowing I wasn't *alone*. That was the flip side of loss.

It was like walking through fire and coming out the other side. You weren't unscathed, but you learned what you could live through. It was a mixed blessing.

"I understand," I murmured.

At that moment, I felt something invisible stitch between us, a fragile thread of understanding.

"How about this?" Haven suggested. "You go ahead and move in."

I didn't mind the abrupt shift in conversation. I knew well the awkwardness of covering the ground of a loss and the need to move on quickly. If you got caught in it, it was like walking through quicksand. Not that I'd ever walked through quicksand. In hindsight, that fell on the list of childhood fears that seemed ridiculously overblown. To deal with loss, you had to keep moving, or you ran the risk of getting mired in it. That's not to say you avoided it, but a part of grief was learning to live with it. You incorporated the loss in your heart and carried on.

My mind nudged on track as Haven continued, "And we'll figure out some things for you to do around here. There's more than enough to choose from."

I felt uncertain about this plan, but I also needed a place to stay. I didn't have any income yet. I didn't know why I was being stubborn about it, but I hated asking for help. I knew from my time in therapy after my dad died that my reticence about asking for help was a response to a tragic loss. Or, for me, it was. I carried a deep-seated need to *never* need anyone.

Because if I didn't need anyone, it wouldn't hurt when they were gone. If I didn't need anyone, I could solve everything myself. If I didn't need anyone, I couldn't get hurt again.

"Elsa?" he prompted.

I'd gotten derailed in my thoughts. Again. I had no idea how long this pause had stretched. "Okay," I finally said.

Haven looked down at me, and his quiet chuckle sent a subtle vibration through my body. "Okay then."

I bit the corner of my lip. When his eyes darkened, I convinced myself that it was a fluke. "I really appreciate this."

I'd have to figure out how to deal with my inconvenient reaction to him. It would pass. It *had* to pass. Relationships weren't for me. I couldn't even ponder why I was contemplating relationships with Haven standing here. Much less chemistry, attraction, and all the messy things that came with them.

"Elsa?" Haven prompted.

I blinked up at him. "Uh-huh?"

"When would you like to move in?"

"As soon as I can?" My voice lilted slightly in question.

"Whatever works for you. It's available."

"Is tonight too soon?"

"It's not."

I nearly bounced on my feet, resisting the urge to fling my arms around him in gratitude.

I just wanted a place to *be*. Coming back to Willow Brook had been a scramble. I had job options, but there was the whole matter of finding an actual job. I still didn't fully understand why I felt the need to build something where the old house was, but I did. Maybe because I didn't want it to feel marred by what we lost. If I built something new there, maybe that would change things.

I was drifting away in my thoughts again when Haven dragged me back.

"Elsa?"

"I'm here," I said quickly, as if marking myself in attendance.

A smile teased the corners of his lips, and my belly shimmied in response.

"You are. We don't lock up, so here's the deal," Haven said. "I have to get back to work, and I don't know how much stuff you have. You can move in anytime. The bathroom is across the hall. You're welcome to use the fridge, and you're always welcome to eat with us over at the main resort."

"Oh, that's too much," I said quickly.

"My mom will be offended if you don't," Haven countered. "Feeding people makes her heart happy, and she'll want to mother-hen you."

"Mother-hen me?"

"Fuss over you. Make sure you feel settled. Make sure you feel welcome. All that." He circled his hand in the air, affection flickering in his eyes. I loved that it was so clear he loved his mom.

He turned, heading for the door, and I trailed him. After the fire, this would've been a cramped space for their whole family. But for me? It felt nice. Cozy. Almost like home. Which didn't make a lick of sense. I'd never lived here. Yet somehow, it felt like it was calling me back. This little pocket of Alaska called me back.

As we approached my car, someone stepped out of the main entrance of the resort.

"There you are," the man said.

I knew he had to be one of the brothers because he looked an awful lot like Haven. When he saw me, his brows hitched up, curiosity swirling in his gaze. He stopped in front of us, assessing me for a moment before Haven spoke. "You remember Elsa?"

The man studied me for a second longer before nodding.

"I used to live next door," I offered, trying to remember which of the brothers this was. They looked a lot alike, all dark hair and silver-blue eyes.

Haven tipped his head toward him. "Jude."

Jude arched a brow, then rocked back on his heels. "One of the younger brothers," he said dryly. His light tone was teasing. "And you lived next door." Jude nodded as if to himself. "Tommy told us the goats greeted you."

A laugh rumbled in my throat. "They did."

Haven glanced at me. "She's going to stay in the staff area. In the barn."

"Good plan." Jude crossed his arms, eyeing me. "Are you going to work? Because we could use all the help we can get."

I burst out laughing. "I told Haven I wanted to do something. I don't know what I can do, but I'm happy to help."

"Do you paint?" Jude asked.

"I do. Do you need some painting done?"

"Yes," Jude said instantly. "We have four rooms that need to be painted. In the next four days."

"Tell me where, and I'll take care of it," I said, relieved to have something useful to offer.

Haven narrowed his eyes at Jude. "Elsa might have a job," he pointed out. "That's *not* here. I haven't had a chance to ask her about that."

"Well, that's the plan, but I don't have one yet," I admitted.

Jude tipped his head to the side. "What do you do?"

"I'm a biologist."

"Oh. Cool." Jude nodded. "What kind of biologist?"

I grinned. "My specialty is whales."

Jude blinked. "Your *specialty* is whales?"

"I monitor their migration routes, their breeding…" I waved my hand vaguely. "All that."

"Oh, huh," Haven said.

"Super cool," Jude teased, nudging him with his elbow.

"Whales are amazing," I said.

"They scare me. They're freaking huge." Jude shuddered.

"They *are* big," I agreed. "And Alaska's a great location to monitor them."

"I bet you can get a job with the state," Haven suggested.

"That's my hope." I nodded. "I've put in a few applications." I lifted my hand and literally crossed my fingers. "Fingers crossed."

"Well, good to have you," Jude said. "And honestly, you don't have to paint. I was just, you know…" He shrugged.

"I don't mind painting. I actually like it. It's something I can do, and it has a meditative quality to it, if you know what I mean."

"I do. You don't have to think too hard about it," Haven said.

"Are you going to eat with us tonight?" Jude asked.

When I hesitated, Haven cut in smoothly, "I just told her Mom would take offense if she didn't," he said. "Do you know what she's making tonight?" His gaze shifted to Jude.

"Spaghetti casserole," Jude said immediately. "Because that's what Tommy requested."

"Well, whatever Tommy asks for, he gets," Haven said dryly.

"I bet your mom takes requests from everybody," I said, smiling. Maggie seemed like the kind of person who would be like that.

"Oh, she does," Haven confirmed. "But Tommy usually gets first dibs. Fortunately, he has good taste, although it's a little repetitive."

I giggled. "I think most kids are probably a little repetitive when it comes to food. They like what they like."

"True story," Jude said dryly.

Haven glanced at his brother. "Did you need something from me?"

"I did," Jude said, snapping his fingers. "I need help mounting that last bathroom cabinet, and I can't do it with two hands, so…"

Haven clapped him on the shoulder. "Between us, we have four hands."

Jude rolled his eyes and started toward the resort.

Haven glanced back at me. "You can come in now, or…?"

I shook my head. "I think I'll go get my stuff and then come back. Is that okay?"

"Of course." Haven nodded. "Catch you later. You can park wherever you want, and you don't need a key. You don't have to check in with us or anything. Just go put your stuff away." He hesitated. "But do let me know if you'll be there for dinner."

"Our mom is definitely going to ask," Jude added.

I smiled. "I'll be there."

"Good," Haven said, turning and walking again.

I hesitated for a beat. "Haven?"

He glanced over his shoulder, one brow arching up.

"Thank you," I said simply.

His expression softened, something unreadable flickering in his eyes before he nodded.

"Anytime."

Chapter Nine

HAVEN

"Will Elsa be here tonight?" my mom asked.

"She said she would."

Cole came walking into the kitchen at that moment. "Will who be here?" he asked.

"Elsa. She's staying in the apartment above the barn. I'm so glad she's back in town." My mom pressed her hand to her chest, letting out a heartfelt sigh. "That sweet girl deserves a happier ending."

Cole caught my eye, his lips curling slightly at the corners. "Of course," he agreed. "When did she move back?"

Tommy came racing into the kitchen. "Yesterday!" he exclaimed. "We found her."

"You found her?" Cole asked, one of his dark brows rising in a slash.

"Yes, she was over on her family's property, and one of the goats knocked her over. Well, specifically, Dolly," I explained.

"There's nothing but a foundation left on that property," Cole pointed out as he crossed the kitchen to snag a slice of cheese off the charcuterie tray.

My mom swatted at his hand. "You're messing up my arrangement," she teased.

"Mom, we're going to eat all this. The minute this tray lands on the table, it'll be a feeding frenzy," he pointed out.

My mom pressed her lips together, casting him a faux glare. "Elsa is coming. We need to behave like civilized people."

"We are civilized," Tommy announced as he skipped across the kitchen, swiping not one but two pieces of cheese off the platter. My mother gave him an indulgent look and lifted the tray high in the air before crossing over to set it on the table.

"It's not like she doesn't know how we live," Cole commented.

"What do you mean?" Tommy asked as he plunked down in a chair, hooking his feet around the legs.

My mom, Cole, and I all looked at each other before she finally said, "She stayed here once before."

"After her father passed away," I added.

Tommy's eyes widened a little. "Well, that's a little sad."

"It is. Sometimes people go through hard things," I replied.

When Tommy had questions about what happened to his mom and dad, how I had adopted him, and how the rest of the family fit together, we'd set him up with a therapist to help us explain. The primary take-home point we learned was to share information in clear, simple terms.

Tommy, like most kids, was full of questions about everything. I didn't know if he would bombard Elsa with them. I hoped not. Because, well, fuck. Talk about a loaded topic. Elsa's dad had died, and Tommy's mom had died, and both of our families lost our homes in a wildfire.

"Where are Jude, Asher, and Grady?" Cole asked as he fetched glasses from the kitchen cabinet and set them on the table.

Our family dinners tended to be slightly chaotic as to who would show up and when. "Jude texted he'd be here, but Asher and Grady are in town," I explained.

"Right here!" Jude said in a singsong voice as he walked into the kitchen. "It's official. I finished mounting all the bathroom cabinets. Do you think Elsa's really going to help paint?"

Jude crossed over to sit at the table while Cole began setting plates out. That was his unofficial task most nights.

"She said she would. I don't see why she wouldn't," I replied.

"Elsa's going to paint?" Tommy looked up. "I wanted to paint."

My mom ruffled his hair. "You have other chores. And school," she pointed out. "Let Elsa paint."

"Okay," Tommy said easily. For the most part, he was an easygoing kid.

Although the rest of us all carried scars from the fire and losing Tommy's mom and our dad, Tommy didn't remember any of it because he was born in the midst of his mother's passing. When it came to loss and grief, that turned out to be a blessing.

Just then, the chime for the main entrance echoed from the front into the kitchen.

"Oh, that must be Elsa!" My mom spun around, hurrying out of the kitchen toward the front.

Knowing Elsa was about to appear sent a sizzle of anticipation through me. I didn't need to be distracted by Elsa, and I was seriously starting to doubt the wisdom of offering her a place to stay.

"Sweetie, you look so good!" My mom walked into the kitchen with Elsa a moment later. She slipped her hand through Elsa's elbow and squeezed, smiling up at her.

"Thank you." Elsa's cheeks were a little pink, and she looked uncertain. An unfamiliar sense of protectiveness rose inside me.

"You know all the boys." My mom gestured to Jude, Cole, Tommy, and me. Tommy waved as he finished chewing whatever he'd just tossed into his mouth. I'd discovered that little boys were bottomless vessels when it came to food. Tommy ate whatever was in front of him. He wasn't picky. He liked everything. Even if he thought something was so-so, he would still eat it.

My mom released Elsa's elbow, hurrying over to check something in the oven. "We are having spaghetti casserole tonight. Tommy loves it."

"We all love it," Jude said with an exaggerated brow waggle.

"It sounds delicious," Elsa offered politely. She looked nervous, and I wanted to assure her the last thing she needed to worry about was being nervous around my family.

My mom was a collector of strays. Not too many, but she liked to mother people. Ever since Bree had died, that urge seemed to grow stronger. Maybe she couldn't save Bree, but she wanted to take care of anyone who crossed her path and needed a little extra love.

"You can sit wherever you want, Elsa. Tommy's in his favorite chair, and the rest of us just sit wherever," my mom explained.

Elsa hesitated. I caught Cole's eyes. He promptly plunked down in a chair beside Tommy. I sensed Elsa was waiting to follow our lead. I took a seat, but Elsa still waited. Jude belatedly picked up the cue and sat down beside me, and Elsa finally took the chair across from me.

"How's Dolly?" she asked, glancing toward Tommy.

He beamed. "She's great. I'm sure she's sorry that she knocked you over. She was just so excited to see you the other day."

Elsa bit her lip as she laughed. "I'm sure that was it."

My mom clucked. "Dolly loves people, and she does get a little excited when she sees them. Tommy can take you on a tour of the rescue program. That's where he works after school most afternoons."

———

I lay in the darkness that night, feeling like the ceiling was mocking me. When we'd stayed here after the fire, my mom had put glow-in-the-dark stars on the ceilings of every bedroom, her small way of trying to find some whimsy in the midst of a tidal wave of loss. I chuckled to myself. This room had the Big Dipper twinkling in the darkness.

Constellations aside, I couldn't sleep tonight. Elsa danced along the edges of my thoughts.

Only one wall separated us, and I could practically feel the force of her presence vibrating through it.

Chapter Ten

ELSA

The frosty grass crunched under my footsteps as I walked through the field toward my family's property. I kept trying to force my brain to call it *my* property, but I hadn't gotten there yet. After the old house burned down, my mother had deeded the property to me. Ever since my dad passed away, she claimed she knew she didn't want to return. All the while, I'd missed Alaska the whole time we were gone.

This morning, I'd woken early in my little room above the barn, marveling at how well I had slept. Sleep had been an elusive, tricky thing for most of my life. I understood the intellectual reasons behind why. Growing up with the chronic presence of uncertainty had been exhausting. It was also confusing because my father was a loving man. He'd just had some offbeat ideas about life that made it feel topsy-turvy.

So many of my childhood memories were blurry as if obscured by sheer fabric blowing in the wind. After my dad died with me right there, crying while I didn't know how to help, my mom had gotten me in to see a therapist. She helped me understand that childhood memories can be muddled and confusing. She explained that even clear memories are tricky because they were filtered through the lens of emotion, and emotion colors everything.

I reached the edge of the field and opened a gate I didn't recall being there. Maggie had told me where to find it. When I'd stopped by the main resort for coffee, she'd offered to walk over with me, but I needed to do this myself.

I adored Maggie. It was hard not to. She was loving and kind and seemed to have a sixth sense of what someone was going through. As soon as Tommy heard the tail-end of our conversation, he had volunteered to come with me. Maggie had narrowed her eyes and reminded him he had school. I sensed Tommy loved to tag along on any jaunt.

I suspected my father had put the gate there. That was the kind of thing he would do, and he'd always worried about anyone coming on our property. He'd been mildly suspicious of everyone. The trees were a mix of blue spruce with a few cottonwoods along the edge where the forest opened up to my property. The landscape glittered under the rising sun as it angled across the frosty ground. The fireweed flowers were still pink, though I knew the blooms could only last through a few more frosts like this. I stopped at the edge of the trees, looking ahead.

In my memory, the house was there. But now, there was just a little grassy rise. From here, I couldn't even see the remnants of the foundation. For a moment, a surge of anxiety rolled through me. I wanted to build a house, my very own, and somehow make this place mine, but that was such a big project. That sense of panic started to churn inside me, like a little motor in my chest spinning out of control.

I forced myself to start moving, to ground myself in my body. When the panic kept building, I came to an abrupt stop and began doing jumping jacks. If anyone saw me doing this, they'd think I was insane. But somehow, the motion settled me quickly.

You're here because you wanted to be here. Dad is gone, and you can't change what happened.

I hated that my father's death, so pointless, tinged my memories and loomed so large. But then, I'd felt helpless over those weeks when he was so sick. He'd ignored my mother's pleas to go to the doctor. She never could've known he'd essentially drown in his lungs from pneumonia the day she drove to town, and I'd be alone with him when it happened.

My mother shaped me with her love for my father, even though she didn't agree with some of his thinking, her resilience, her love for wildlife, and this place. I was a wildlife biologist because of her. We'd watch the beluga whales sometimes along Turnagain Arm. Belugas were flashes of white in the blue water, and I loved watching them swim.

I took a slow breath, the air crisp and fresh, carrying hints of the ocean and mingling with the sharp scent of evergreen. An eagle's call pierced the air. I glanced around to see one gliding low over the rise where the foundation was. It landed on an old utility pole, now broken in half. I watched as it folded its big wings into its sides, then looked around the landscape like it owned it. I suppose it did.

I kept walking toward the foundation. The eagle watched me curiously. Having grown up in Alaska, I was accustomed to eagles. They were everywhere here, and I loved them. Something was so powerful about them. This eagle was entirely unperturbed by my presence. I stopped nearby. All the while, the bird just kept looking at me.

Standing in the old foundation, I spun in a slow circle, looking at the ground, trying to figure out which room would have been where. The house had faced Heartfire Falls.

Back then, I couldn't see the resort through the trees, but the fire had burned away the taller trees. I vaguely remembered what the old resort looked like, but I hadn't been there too often.

My mom had always told me that if I needed anything, I should go get Maggie. She'd helped me that afternoon when my father died. I'd called her with shaking hands.

I paused where I thought the living room had been, where my dad had taken his last labored breath on the couch after resting for weeks.

Everything suddenly felt tight inside. The stab of grief was piercing, stealing my breath for a moment. My tears, as they fell, cooled almost instantly in the chilly morning air. It wasn't as if I hadn't cried enough.

I lifted my eyes, feeling the eagle's gaze on me. Maybe it was crazy, but I could have sworn it somehow understood. I felt a sense of kinship with this fierce-looking bird.

Scanning the horizon again, I remained startled at the bold beauty of Alaska's landscape.

"He's not coming back," I said to the wind and the trees and the eagle.

I knew that. Even though I'd had times when I'd felt crazy with grief, I'd never thought my dad could come back. But I had wondered if I would get here and feel his presence.

All I felt was a sense of calm. Not quite peace, but a quiet certainty that I was finally where I was supposed to be again.

After one more deep breath, I glanced at the eagle. I felt my lips curl into a smile as I studied the bird. "Thanks for the company."

Of course, the eagle had nothing to say in return. As I walked back toward Heartfire Falls, I felt a little lighter inside. The trepidation of coming here again had eased. When I got to the gate, I left it open behind me. I made a mental note to ask Haven if I could just tear it down. I didn't want it to be there. I wanted to erase the boundaries my dad had built around our life.

This time, I didn't angle straight back toward the new resort. Instead, I crossed the small rise and headed toward Heartfire Falls. I used to sneak over there when I was a little girl.

I passed by the resort on one side and could see the property where they had the rescue program, which I was curious about. My memory led me to the waterfall even though I wasn't sure I could find it. I followed a trail through some trees until I could hear the falls rushing. I reached the river first, smiling at the bluish water. This river branched off from a bigger river fed by a glacier.

The rushing water grew louder as I approached, and I felt a smile break across my face. As soon as I turned onto the path, the clearing opened. A pool was at the base of the falls, with water cascading over the rocks.

This memory was clear. I loved it here.

I stepped to the edge of the pool before skirting around to walk along the rocks behind the falls. That had been my favorite thing when I was little. It was a rock shelf that seemed magically dry to me as a child.

It was past the season when the salmon were running, but when the time was right, they swam right over this waterfall into the pool below, hence its popularity as a tourist destination for fishing. As I came back out from behind the falls, I let out a little squeak when I saw Haven standing on the other side of the pool.

"Didn't mean to scare you," he called.

"I hope it's okay I'm here," I called in return, slipping back from the rock ledge to round the water at the base of the falls.

"Of course, it's okay," he said easily.

"I told your mom I might walk over here," I said, as if I had to explain myself.

Haven tipped his head to the side. "Totally fine. You don't have to report your whereabouts. You're staying here, so come to the falls all you want."

I smiled up at him, feeling a giddy sense of joy. Even though he was being kind and polite, I had already picked up that he was a little taciturn, giving off a vibe of carrying the entire world on his shoulders. But then, I suppose he shouldered a lot. He was the oldest of the brothers and probably had to pick up so many pieces after the fire.

"Thank you again for offering to let me stay here." I had to hold back from giving him a hug, which was probably for the best, because I also *totally* had the hots for him. Even though this hug wasn't about that. "I walked over to our property this morning. I don't know how I'm going to do it, but I'm going to build a house," I announced, as if saying it firmly enough would will it to fruition.

A little glint entered his gaze. "You'll figure it out. We can probably help with a plan for that and even help build it."

"Huh?" I blurted out.

"Well, we didn't build this resort ourselves because it's pretty freaking big, but we're all handy. We'll help with whatever you want."

"Okay." I eyed him skeptically. "I think you're kind of busy, Haven. And it's a long shot. I know it won't happen soon. Step one: get a job. That's as far as I've gotten in my planning," I said dryly.

He nodded, his eyes dipping down as he idly scuffed the toe of his boot on the ground.

"Did you follow me because you saw me?" I asked.

"I saw someone walking through the trees, but I didn't realize it was you. That's all. I love coming here. It's one of my favorite places."

"I used to sneak over here when I was a kid. I figure I can fess up now. You know, asking forgiveness rather than permission. Oh, years later." I waved airily toward the waterfall.

When he smiled and chuckled, I felt like I'd won something and almost clapped my hands. "It wouldn't have mattered. People were always here at the falls when the resort was open. I'm surprised you managed to sneak anywhere. My mom's back at the house making breakfast for you."

"What? She doesn't need to make me breakfast. Haven, you need to tell her she doesn't have to cook for me all the time."

"I'm not going to tell her that."

"Why?"

"Because it makes her happy. So humor me."

Chapter Eleven

HAVEN

The following day

Elsa's voice reached me from down the hall. "What do you think?"

I tried to ignore the way my pulse kicked up at the sound of her voice.

"You can pick whatever colors you want, Elsa," Jude replied.

I stopped in the doorway to see her standing there. She wore an oversized T-shirt and leggings with paint smeared on her cheek. Her hair was pulled up in a messy bun with what appeared to be a broken pen stuck through it.

"What do you think?" she asked, glancing over at me.

I was too distracted by how cute she looked to say a word.

"Haven?" Jude prompted.

Giving myself a mental shake, I glanced at the wall in question. "It looks great."

Elsa rested one hand on her hip, her arms and hands covered in paint. "I'm going with mostly neutral colors, but every room has an accent wall." She gestured with the paint roller toward what I presumed was the accent wall.

"Awesome."

"Really?" Her brow arched up in skepticism.

"Totally awesome," Jude chimed in.

"I mean it," I insisted.

"You guys are no help."

I chuckled. "We're just happy you're helping, Elsa."

"I should be done by the end of the week. I decided to keep it simple and pick the accent wall for every room first, then go through the rest. I'm under budget, according to your mom," she said.

Jude flashed me a grin before clapping Elsa on the shoulder as he walked past her. "It looks great." He left the room, tossing over his shoulder, "I'm headed over to the rescue program. They called me about needing some help with a new fence, so I'm going to help put that up. I'll be back in a while."

That left me alone with Elsa, who had already started rolling paint onto the wall again. I watched as she systematically made her way up and down.

"Thank you for asking me to do this. I forgot that I actually love painting. It's very soothing."

"Yeah?"

She cast a quick smile over her shoulder. "Yes. It's almost meditative. I used to do it in college. Side job. That and waiting tables. Painting didn't give me tips, but it was more relaxing. Peace and quiet. Nobody bothers you. But waiting tables brought home the bacon, so to speak."

"Where did you go to college?" I was way too curious about her.

"University of Washington. That's where I got my marine biology degree and then my master's. They have a great program there."

"I would imagine. There are lots of orcas there."

Her smile turned wistful. "And here too. As I mentioned, whales are my specialty."

"Well, there are plenty of those in Alaska."

"There are." She kept rolling paint and sighed.

"Didn't you mention you have an interview?"

"I do. It's tomorrow, so I won't be able to paint in the morning."

"You're going to ace it."

She finished one wall and glanced over at me. "That's nice of you to say, but I don't know."

"I do," I said with confidence because I meant it.

I didn't know a lot about Elsa beyond that she'd been our neighbor and then my high school crush.

"I know you're a hard worker. You're up here, all on your own. That counts for something."

"Really?"

"It matters in Alaska. I bet you know all the things about the whales here."

She pressed her lips together. "What do *you* know about marine biology?"

I paused, pressing my tongue in my cheek. "That you monitor migration patterns and track things."

When she giggled, my heart squeezed tight, and it felt as if that connection between us—one I didn't even fully understand—tightened.

"I'll let you know how it goes, although I probably won't know tomorrow. Who knows how many applicants they have."

"Wouldn't hurt you to be optimistic," I offered, my voice low.

She rolled her eyes. "Says you."

"What do you mean?"

"You're cynical. More cynical than me, which is saying something." Her tone was as dry as ash, with an eye roll to boot.

My laugh came out unexpectedly as I shook my head. "Okay, fair point. Also, you don't have to report to me about your schedule. Or to any of us."

She rested her hand on her hip again. "I don't want to keep arguing with you about this. I need to help. It's important. I have to contribute something, and I like painting."

"I know. But if you didn't do it, it would be okay."

She held my gaze long enough that every cell in my body fired before she turned away and began rolling paint on the wall. I had to force my feet to leave the room when all I wanted to do was linger and watch Elsa paint. But that wasn't rational. She was a distraction. A delectable distraction.

———

That night, I walked through the darkness, listening to the rustle of the wind in the trees, an owl calling into the night with another answering. When I walked upstairs, Elsa was sitting on the couch. Her hair was up in another messy bun, and she was wearing sweatpants and a tank top. When she smiled at me, it was impossible not to smile back.

"Hey." Her voice was warm.

Just one word was enough to amp up the anticipation humming in my veins.

"Hey." My voice came out gruff, and I resisted the urge to clear my throat.

"I hope it's okay that I'm watching TV." She gestured toward the screen.

"Of course. You live here."

Elsa tipped her head to the side. "I'm *staying* here."

I didn't know why, but her insistence on making that distinction elicited a wave of protectiveness. "You *live* here," I repeated. "Why do you insist on saying you're just staying here?"

I left my boots by the door and hung up my jacket, a sense of trepidation sliding through me as I crossed the room. My draw to her was so strong, I wanted to sit down on the couch beside her and curl my arm around her shoulders.

And what, dude? Are you pretending to play house here?

I forced myself to take the chair instead, keeping a little distance from her.

Elsa studied me for a moment before shrugging. "I don't know. I guess... well, I've only been here two nights, so it feels temporary. Honestly, everything has felt temporary since we moved away."

I wanted to tell her that she belonged here, that she was home. But I kept my mouth shut, even as I felt that truth settle deep inside me.

Elsa shrugged, and I tried not to notice her shoulders. Fuck me, even her shoulders were cute. There was a dusting of freckles on them, and I wanted to count them. I wanted to find every freckle on her curvy body. Instead, I forced myself to look away. "What are you watching?"

When I glanced back at Elsa, her cheeks were pink, and she

pressed her lips together before she giggled. Her fucking giggle was like a lasso around my heart.

"I know reality TV is ridiculous, but I just love it. I never got to watch TV when I was a kid, so I don't think the specialness of it will ever wear off. In these shows, their lives are ridiculous. It's hysterical because it's nothing like my life, so it's fun. They're so dramatic and always arguing over stupid things, and I love it. That's all." She let out a happy little sigh.

My lips kicked up on one side, and a chuckle rumbled in my throat. "Hey, if you love it, enjoy it. I'm a fan of that."

"Of the show?"

"Of you watching a show that you love."

I wanted to ask her so many questions. Just like before, there was an effervescence to Elsa, probably why I'd crushed on her in high school. Her basic nature was sunshiny and cheerful, with almost an innocence to it. My heart twisted in my chest because I knew life wasn't always sunshiny. I also knew Elsa understood that.

"Anyway, back to the temporary thing," she said, her voice softer. "I'm sure you can put the pieces together that moving after my dad passed was hard." Something passed through her gaze, but she shook her head, almost as if she were tossing the thought away. "And before that, it felt like I was just waiting. My dad was kind of funky." She paused as if working through the thoughts in real time. "After we moved, it felt like my life was borrowed. I guess that's how it's felt since." Her voice was softer when she spoke again. "And finally, I realized I needed to come back here. I mean, that property is mine, and it's beautiful. Right?" She nodded to herself, as if I'd questioned it.

"Of course it's beautiful. Alaska is God's country."

A wide smile cracked across her face, and I felt like I'd just given her a present.

"Yes!" she enthused. "It is! I needed to come back because this was the only place that's ever felt like home to me." She let out a soft sigh. "But, I mean, this is your family's place. And you're being really nice, insisting that I don't need to pay rent, and blah, blah, blah." She circled her hand in the air.

Suddenly, the urge to make sure Elsa felt like she belonged howled inside me.

My life hadn't been perfect. We'd had a painful loss, first with my dad, who I'd adored, and then the fire. But I had *always* known where I belonged. Belonging was a sense of place. But I understood it as being connected to my family and all we had together.

"In my opinion, you live here, Elsa."

"Stubborn much?" she teased lightly.

"It's possible I've been accused of that," I said somberly.

She bit her lip as she smiled at me, then lifted a bowl I hadn't even noticed she had in her lap. What with her freckled shoulders, her messy bun, her smile, and those eyes I could get lost in? Well, I didn't catch many other details.

"Do you want some kettle corn?" she asked.

The next thing I knew, I was sitting on the couch beside her, eating kettle corn. And even more shocking, I got sucked right into the drama of the show.

"She's a shit-stirrer," Elsa said at one point, pointing at one of the women on the screen.

"Oh, I can see that. But I think that's part of the job requirement if you will. I mean, they can't just have people living healthy, stable lives. They've got to have stuff happening."

Elsa's messy bun bounced with her enthusiastic nod.

I chuckled again. When I got up and stretched before heading toward my room later, I realized I might have smiled and laughed more since Elsa had been here than I had in years. Even when things were good, even before the fire, I'd had a lot to handle.

Yet again that night, I was deeply aware that Elsa was just on the other side of the wall between our rooms.

So close. Yet so far.

Chapter Twelve

ELSA

My foot bounced where I sat in the waiting room with one leg crossed over my other knee. I was trying not to be nervous, but I was failing. Taking a quick breath, I let it out in a quiet sigh.

You are qualified for this job, Elsa.

The woman at the receptionist's desk called my name. I stood so quickly I almost lost my balance.

"That's me." I practically ran to the desk, catching myself at the last minute and forcing my stride to slow.

"Janie will be right with you." She stood and opened a door beside her desk, leading me down a hallway and into a small conference room. "Go ahead and have a seat." She gestured toward the table. "Would you like some coffee?"

I shook my head quickly. The last thing I needed was more caffeine. "Thank you, though."

Just as I was sitting down, another woman appeared in the doorway. "Hi, you must be Elsa. I'm Janie."

Awkwardly, I immediately stood again. "Yes." Thrusting a hand forward, I shook hers. Her grip was warm, her handshake steady.

"Go ahead and finish having a seat." She chuckled as she closed the door behind her and sat across from me. "How are you?"

Her calm tone and warm eyes eased the tension drawn tight inside me. I *really* wanted this job, and it wasn't just because I needed the money.

Monitoring the beluga whales, tracking their migration patterns, and contributing to conservation efforts was basically a dream job for me. Beyond those main duties, the office here monitored many other local wildlife and helped with any rescues.

By the time my interview was over, I didn't even remember most of my answers. I finished with, "Thank you so much. This is basically a dream job for me, and maybe I'm not supposed to say that, but that's how I feel." My words sounded so earnest that I felt ridiculous once my brain caught up to what I said.

Janie's brown eyes crinkled at the corners with her smile. "I can tell you're passionate about this, and that pretty much makes my day." She looked as if she were pondering what to say next, and I forced myself to keep my mouth shut while I waited. "We'd like to offer you the position."

"We?" I squeaked.

"Well, *me*." Janie laughed softly. "Your credentials and references are excellent. Your education is a great fit, and you were born and raised in Alaska. That, for this, is important. You understand the environment here and the many competing issues we face as wildlife biologists. Your primary role will be the projects around monitoring whales, but that won't be all of your responsibilities by any stretch, and we need someone with that kind of flexibility and interest."

It was all I could do not to jump up and down and shout for joy. Instead, I nodded slowly. "Oh wow. This is amazing! I thought there would be so much competition." I took a deep breath, letting it out in a ragged sigh. Before I knew it, I had dropped my face into my hands, trying to keep from bursting into tears. In this case, it was a mix of happy tears and sheer overwhelmed tears.

"Are you okay?" Janie asked.

I lifted my head, swiping my fingertips across my cheeks. "I'm sorry. I know that's not professional." My voice was watery. "It's just... it's been a lot. Coming home has been a lot."

As I looked at her, I realized she must know my story. I wasn't naive enough to think people didn't do online searches when hiring.

She didn't comment, but her gaze was warm and understanding. "Well, from what you said in your application, you just moved back to town, and this is where you grew up. That would carry a lot of emotion, no matter what."

"Thank you for understanding." Somehow, that little burst of emotion helped me gather myself. "I hope being this unprofessional doesn't make me lose the job offer."

She shook her head. "No, you were our top candidate before you even came in for your interview. You have the most experience specific to this job, which is a specific job. Not to be repetitive, but it fits." She chuckled when I beamed back at her. "I'll introduce you to our HR person on the way out, and she'll get you all set up. When do you want to start?"

"When do I want to start?" I repeated.

She grinned. "Yeah. Officially, this position's funding starts next week, so you can start any day after Monday. But we also realize you may not be ready then. I don't know where you're at with housing and all that, so—"

"I can start Monday." I cut in immediately.

———

As I skipped from my car into the barn, giddiness spun inside me. It felt like a sense of hope was sprouting. I jogged up the stairs to the apartment. I was opening the door, walking through it and not paying any attention when I collided with something solid.

Glancing up, I found Haven stepping back. "Sorry about that."

I was too excited to even think clearly. "I got the job!" I burst out, jumping up and flinging my arms around his shoulders. Thankfully, he had quick reflexes and caught me.

And, sweet hell, Haven gave *excellent* hugs. His embrace was strong and warm.

I kicked my feet up behind me, feeling the rumble of his chuckle against my chest when he spun me around. He was still holding me when I leaned my head back, so caught up in my joy I wasn't even thinking.

"Isn't it awesome?" I exclaimed.

He chuckled again, and the sound vibrated through me. As if we recognized at the same time that he held me in a full-on embrace, we both fell quiet. Heat blazed into my cheeks, and I took a quick breath.

"Okay, maybe that was weird," I suddenly said.

"Being excited that you got a job? Your dream job?" he prompted, still holding me close.

I didn't want him to put me down. I liked being this close to Haven. A lot.

I took another shaky breath. "I kind of flung myself at you."

His lips curled at the corners, and my belly did a little shimmy, tingles radiating throughout my body.

"I guess I can catch." He slowly lowered me to the floor before stepping back.

I ignored the sharp pang of disappointment and forced myself to take another step away.

"We should celebrate. Tell me what kind of food you want, and we'll have it for dinner."

"Huh?"

"You know, celebrate that you got a job?" Haven eyed me curiously.

Maybe it wasn't obvious to him that celebrating little events like this wasn't something I was used to. "Oh, um, we should celebrate?"

"Absolutely," he said firmly. "What's your favorite food?"

I blinked, biting my lip. "I don't know."

"You don't know?"

"I love cheese. Like, when your mom made that charcuterie board? That was amazing. And... I've never had homemade mac and cheese, but I've heard it's really good."

"Okay. We're definitely having mac and cheese, and my mom will probably make a lot more."

"I don't want your mom to put herself out."

Haven rolled his eyes and took a step back in my direction, placing his big hands on my shoulders. I thrilled at the feel of his touch, heat flaring in my cheeks again.

"You're not putting her out. Or anyone. That's what we do here. We celebrate small wins, and this is bigger than small. It's your dream job, and you freaking got it."

A giggle slipped out. "I know. I kind of can't believe it."

He startled me by dipping his head and giving me a quick kiss. "Fucking believe it."

We stared at each other. Once again, it seemed as if we both realized what had just happened. It wasn't like that was a sexy kiss or anything, but it was *still* a kiss, and my lips burned from it.

"I'll see you at dinner tonight." He lifted his hand for a high five, and I slapped my palm to his, the heat of his touch flashing up my arm.

He hurried past me, closing the door behind him and leaving me upstairs by myself. I pressed two fingers to my lips, almost as if I could catch his kiss and hold it there. I was hot all over, ablaze with awareness and sensation.

I didn't know how long I stood there until my phone chirped in my pocket, and I nearly jumped at the sound.

Chapter Thirteen

HAVEN

Thank fuck, I was busy. That hug, followed by *that* kiss—which I hadn't intended to be sexual—was burned on my lips. The second my mouth met the soft give of Elsa's plump lips, it had been like a bolt of lightning sizzling through my body, the hot shock of it still burning hours later.

But we had a crazy day, like every day, and its relentless pace kept me distracted. We were in a hustle to finish the work at the main resort. I threw myself into one task after another, blowing through work with such focus that when Cole stopped by, he let out a low whistle. "Damn, bro. You're kicking some ass on the work today."

I tossed my tool bag on the ground, dragging my sleeve across my forehead. "A few finishing touches out here, that's it." Part of the renovations meant sprucing up the downstairs area of the old barn to store gear for the various trips we guided. I'd spent a few hours finishing up the shelving out here.

"We should have Elsa do some painting on the outside of this barn. Make it look good," Cole said as he leaned his shoulder on the inside of the doorway.

"You think?" I prompted.

"She's done a great job with the painting. The rooms look good. On the outside, where the old sign was, she could paint the name, that kind of thing. She seems all worried about making sure she earns her 'keep,'" he added with air quotes and a chuckle. "You okay?"

"Yeah, I'm fine. Why do you ask?" I countered quickly, not about to admit that the mere mention of Elsa's name set fire to burning on my lips again.

It was just a kiss. Just a friendly, congratulatory kind of thing, or so my brain tried to convince me. If it could speak, my body had nothing more than a sly laugh in response to that.

"Mom's going crazy in the kitchen, by the way," Cole added. "She said something about Elsa getting her dream job, and we're doing a buffet celebration."

I grinned. "I texted Mom. I ran into Elsa after her job interview, and she was all excited because she got the job."

Cole nodded, his gaze sobering. "Nice! I'm guessing it was hard when they moved away. I'm glad she came home. She might as well make Alaska hers again, you know?"

I scuffed my boot on the floor under my heel. "Yeah."

"Mom's beside herself," he added. "Gives her somebody to fuss over." Cole let out a little sigh. "We all miss Bree. And there is kind of a shortage of women around here. I mean, hell, there's—"

He was cut off abruptly when Tommy came barreling into the barn, letting out a whoop with two goats chasing him. Cole and I chuckled together.

Tommy was a boy through and through, wild and full of energy. Thank God we lived out here, where he had plenty of ways to burn off his energy. If we didn't, I think he'd drive us all batshit crazy.

As it was, we still had to keep him on point. "Hey, bud," I said when he stopped beside me after looping around us in a circle. I ruffled his hair. "How'd school go today?"

"Good. The teacher says she's gonna call you."

"How come?"

"I guess I have trouble sitting still."

"You *guess*?" Cole snorted.

I eyed the purple fading in Tommy's hair, which was growing out. "Sitting still is definitely not your strength."

Tommy let out a dramatic sigh. "I know."

"But you gotta figure it out, dude. We all do," Cole added.

"Fine," Tommy replied enthusiastically.

"You taking care of your chores? The stuff over the rescue program?" I asked as the three of us began walking together from the barn over to the main house.

"Of course. The bus drops me off there, and I do that first."

"I know, just double-checking," I said.

"What's for dinner?" Tommy asked. That was always an important question for him.

Cole teased, "Your grandma is making a buffet because Elsa got her job."

"Ooh, a buffet?" At that, Tommy started running.

I laughed, shaking my head. "Not even that old and I can't keep up with him," I said as I glanced toward Cole.

"You're an oldie, dude." He quipped, nudging me with his shoulder as we walked.

Our mom was not shy about celebrating anything, and she'd gone all out for Elsa. There was the gooiest mac and cheese *ever*, according to my mom, along with braised caribou, one of her Brussels sprout casseroles, mashed potatoes, and a generous charcuterie board.

Elsa looked abashed when she sat at the table a little later. "I can't believe you did all this for me, Maggie."

"Honey, you got a job, and Haven said that you said it was your dream job. I'm thrilled for you," my mom replied.

Elsa pressed her lips together. "I just don't want you to feel like you have to go out of your way for me like this."

"Honey, we celebrate things here. Get used to it," my mom said firmly.

My heart twisted a little because Elsa looked as if she felt adrift. Celebrating anything didn't seem like something she was accustomed to. Maybe I didn't know all the details about her family life, but I knew her dad had kept things simple to the extreme.

When she looked over at my mom, I thought there was a sheen of tears in her eyes for a second, but she blinked and glanced down at her plate. "Thank you." Her smile was tremulous when she met my mom's eyes again.

"All right, who's going to say grace?" my mom asked.

Tommy raced through grace. "For this food, in a world where many walk in hunger. For our faith, in a world where many walk in fear. For this fellowship, in a world where many walk alone. We give thanks."

After he finished, Elsa glanced over at Tommy. "I like that blessing a lot."

"It's the only one I know." Tommy shrugged.

My mom smiled over at Tommy. "My mom always said that one. It's been passed down in her family. I don't know officially where it came from, but it's perfect. We don't make it to church often, but to me, that little blessing captures what matters in the world."

Elsa was completely quiet for a moment before she nodded. "It does."

"Now eat up, hon." My mom beamed at her.

When Elsa giggled at that, hot damn, it felt like she swung a lasso across the table and cinched it tight around my heart.

Dinner with my family involved a lot of conversation, ranging from mundane to casual jokes to business. These days, we had lots of logistics to cover. We were racing toward the deadline we'd set for ourselves to reopen the resort.

"We've got that computer system up and running," my mom said. "I feel clunky with it, but it seems simple. We even have a little point-of-sale thing with a calendar. People can make their own reservations, but we have to confirm them. We need to hire someone for that."

"For what?" Elsa prompted.

"Handling this online stuff. I can do the kitchen and handle the guests, but I'm on the information cow-path, so all this computer stuff feels overwhelming." My mom eyed Elsa with hope in her eyes.

"I'll try to help. I'm pretty nifty with computer stuff. I'm starting my job next week, and I'll be painting, but I'll take a look and make sure it's all lined up. If you'd like help hiring for that, I'm happy to do that too," Elsa offered.

"I think we should hire someone, and I'd love any help you can give." The tension lining my mother's face eased, her relief clear.

"Mom, it's going to be fine," Cole said, the most easygoing of all of us.

When Elsa looked over at my mom, genuine concern in her gaze, my heart twisted. She wanted to help. She wanted to make my mom feel okay, and that meant the world to me.

Throughout dinner, I was quieter than usual because I almost didn't trust myself around Elsa. Just having her there was stretching my nerves.

Fuck me.

I was glad she came back to Willow Brook. But holy hell, I was going to have to get a grip. Surely, this was just some kind of fluke. I'd figured that old high school crush was long gone. Instead, all she had to do was appear, like she was a veritable ray of sun in my world. Cheerful, kind, pushy about wanting to help, and delectably sexy. The only thing between us at night was a thin wall.

I mentally shook myself. *Get a fucking grip. You have other priorities.*

Chapter Fourteen

ELSA

My thoughts were obnoxious. I kept replaying that kiss with Haven, telling myself it was just a heat-of-the-moment thing. Inconveniently, most of me wanted it to mean more. I wanted Haven to feel the way I did. Although, I didn't even *know* how I felt. Desire wasn't something I had much experience with or, frankly, time to consider.

"Honey, you don't have to help with the dishes," Maggie said, interrupting my train of thought about Haven.

"I want to," I replied. "Thank you so much for this."

"For what?"

"I just got a job. You didn't have to do a big celebration."

Maggie pressed her lips together as she untied her apron and hung it on a hook by the pantry door.

"Elsa, I cook dinner every night. I love to have a reason to celebrate anything." Her gaze sobered as she studied me quietly. I put the last dish in the dishwasher and closed it, feeling unsettled, my belly jumbled with uncertainty.

"I'm guessing you didn't celebrate many things growing up at your house."

Emotion knotted in my throat. I cleared it, took a slow breath, and shook my head. "No, not really."

"If you ever want to talk, I'm here."

I looked at this warm and kind woman who had been through so much of her own loss. As a little girl, I remembered feeling lonely and out of place, making up stories about families in my head. The Silvers and Heartfire Falls had been the pinnacle of what I imagined a family should be. Six rowdy boys, one girl, and two loving parents.

Those were the details I had pieced together about them. Of all the kids, Bree was the only one who ever happened to see me in Heartfire Falls when I used to sneak over. She had been kind and told me I could come over anytime.

So much had changed for them. Their father had died. Then Bree. And now, Maggie was worrying about me.

"Maggie—" I twisted my hands together and drew in a sharp breath. "I'm okay. Things were fine after we moved. I loved my dad. He was just..." Pausing, I tried to think of the right words. "So into his off-the-grid life. He took it a smidge too far," I offered with a little eye roll.

Maggie laughed softly. "You seem more than okay. I know what it's like to sometimes be okay, but also have bad days and just need someone to listen. So I'm here if you ever need that." She paused, appearing to consider her words. "Your dad loved you very much."

I blinked away the tears stinging my eyes. Before I could say anything else, Maggie crossed the kitchen and pulled me into a comforting hug. When she stepped back, she placed her hands on my shoulders and squeezed. "There's nothing you could have done, and there's no sense in even thinking that. You're not allowed to beat yourself up for overthinking things that you can't change," she said firmly.

A little laugh sputtered out. "It helps to be reminded."

Maggie stepped back. "Sometimes we end up in situations we don't know how to remedy. When that happens, we do the best we can. I don't think your mom knew how sideways it could go when your father got sick. And I'm so, so sorry you had to be there for it."

My grief around this felt old, like a stone worn smooth. "They sent me to therapy, you know. I definitely understand that I can't change the past. I can't undo it. I just have to learn to live with it."

"I'm glad you came back," she said softly.

"I needed to. I've missed Alaska ever since we moved."

She reached out, tapping her fingertips under my chin lightly. "That's how it should be. Sometimes a place holds something for us. No matter how much you talk yourself into worrying, you are welcome here and always will be." I felt her words in my heart and knew she meant them.

Tommy came skidding into the kitchen, abruptly snapping through the moment. "Grandma!"

Maggie glanced down at him, ruffling his hair. "Yes?"

"I'm out of toothpaste."

She chuckled. His interruption was the perfect way to lighten what had become an emotionally loaded conversation. "All right, let's go find you a new tube of toothpaste."

Tommy glanced over at me. "Happy get-a-new-job day, Elsa," he announced with a wide smile.

"Thank you." I waved goodnight and slipped out of the main resort to walk over to the barn.

I'd forgotten how beautiful the stars were in Alaska. There was almost no light pollution out here, so the stars glittered with brightness. My breath misted in the air as I stopped along the small rise between the resort and the barn. Leaning my head back, I felt wide open inside.

"Wow," I breathed to the sky.

The stars appeared so close, as if I could reach up and hold one in my hand.

When I was little, we'd go out and look at the stars whenever we could, and my dad would point out the constellations to me. Now, it felt like the stars were watching over me.

I resumed walking, my footsteps crunching on the frosty ground. As I walked up the stairs, I wondered if Haven was here. The apartment was quiet when I walked in, and Haven's room was dark with the door left open, so I assumed he was out.

Why are you so worried about where Haven is?

My lips burned from the memory of that brief kiss when my mind taunted me.

It wasn't a romantic kiss, I told myself for what felt like the thousandth time.

With a sigh, I quickly went through the motions of getting ready for bed. I heard Haven come in after I was in my bedroom, but I stayed quiet. It didn't matter that there was a thin wall between my room and his. It didn't matter that I knew his bed was against the same wall as my bed.

I almost groaned aloud at how ridiculous my train of thought was. Against the odds with my body churning restlessly, I fell asleep.

During the night, my bladder woke me, and I tiptoed into the shared bathroom. I was a little groggy and out of it. The tiny nightlight by the sink gave me just enough light to see.

A moment later, I walked out, stopping in the kitchen to get a sip of water. Setting the glass on the counter, I turned, only to collide with a tall, muscular man. Haven.

My palm landed on his bare chest. "Oh!" I exclaimed.

My eyes collided with his. His eyes widened slightly in surprise. Neither one of us moved.

Chapter Fifteen

ELSA

As I stood there, a tiny corner of my brain shouted that I was wearing a tank top and the little cotton shorts I liked sleeping in. They were soft and stretchy and so comfortable. Meanwhile, my brain also clocked that Haven was shirtless and wearing a pair of fitted boxer briefs.

Even in my sleep-hazed mind, I managed to absorb that his chest was pure muscle with a dusting of hair. He emanated heat, and it felt as if it spun around me in a soft caress. Sweet hell. Haven, with that dark hair rumpled from sleep and a day or two's growth of stubble, just might have been the most delicious, sexy sight I'd ever encountered.

"Elsa," he finally said, his voice a little ragged on the edges with sleep.

"I was just using the bathroom and getting some water," I said, my hand still on his chest as I gestured behind me with the other one pointlessly.

Why else would anyone be out here in the middle of the night?

He nodded wordlessly, and we just kept staring at each other. I couldn't make myself move away.

"Thanks for my get-a-job celebration," I added, instantly feeling silly.

I stood here close to naked, inches away from him, with my hand on his chest, which was warm and muscly, and I was thanking him.

His dark eyes studied me as his lips kicked up at one corner. The following moment felt like molasses dropping off a spoon in a slow, delicious roll. He stepped incrementally closer, even though it didn't really feel like he moved, or maybe I moved.

I could barely breathe, and my pulse was racing at a breakneck pace. So fast, I was convinced my heart might pound its way out of my chest. I could feel his own heart beating under my palm.

"Elsa," Haven whispered as he dipped his head.

This time, when I felt the hot shock of his lips on mine, I let out a little whimper. *All* of me was leaning toward him.

My fingers flexed against his chest. When he slid one hand into my hair and angled my head to the side to deepen our kiss, I moaned. In the next moment, there was no doubt he stepped closer to me. He slid his other arm around my waist, his palm splaying just over the top of my bottom, and he brought me flush against every hard inch of his body.

I gasped into our kiss at the feel of his arousal pressing against my lower belly. My nipples were tight, and all of me was dizzy with need, with desire, with a rushing want.

I just wanted *more*—of this kiss, of Haven, of all of it. I curled my arm around his waist, savoring the corded muscles along his back as he deepened our kiss, his tongue claiming my mouth, my own teasing with his. This wasn't my first kiss, but I'd always felt a little detached. I'd honestly never grasped the whole chemistry thing. Kisses usually let me down.

Kisses from Haven were the opposite. This was like being dropped into sensation, a fire burning up inside me. At some point, his knee nudged between my thighs, and before I could even think it through, I was rocking my hips over his thigh.

We broke apart, our breaths heaving in the quiet room.

"Elsa." My name fell into the space between us.

The air felt loaded, cinders drifting into that charged space, the heat building.

"Elsa," Haven rasped again.

I didn't quite know what I wanted, but I *absolutely* didn't want this to end. Not yet.

"Tell me what you want, sweetheart."

His words rumbled over me, and I shocked myself by saying, "You."

He took a small step back, lifting my hips onto the counter. He rested both hands beside my hips while my legs dangled down, his eyes boring into mine in the darkness.

When he pressed hot kisses down the side of my neck, I shivered against him, his name a ragged plea. I was burning up, heat rising so swiftly inside that it felt as if my skin couldn't contain it. My nerve endings were sparking.

Haven stilled, resting his hands on either side of my hips. "Elsa."

I could see the glimmer of blue in his eyes in the mostly dark room with nothing more than the ambient light cast from above the stove where a small light shined. "What do you want?" he whispered.

I placed a palm on his chest, savoring the warmth. He felt alive, his body humming with electricity. I could feel the rapid kick of his heart against my palm, and relief slipped through me to discover his heart was racing as fast as mine.

"Just kiss me," I whispered in reply.

When his lips hitched slightly at one corner, my belly shimmied. In a fiery second, he fit his mouth over mine again, and I sighed with sheer relief, neediness, and more. There was a push and pull inside me. The relief at finally giving in to this softened me, while the desire raced at a breakneck pace, gathering force, hurtling forward.

His tongue glided against mine, his kiss alternately masterful and gentle. One of his hands slid into my hair, his palm dragging down. I felt his fingers press at the base of my neck and shivered all over at the feel of it. I couldn't get close enough, and as the fiery seconds ticked by, I plastered myself to him. Through the thin cotton of my tank top, a nuisance between us, I could feel the heat of his skin.

My hand slid around his waist, savoring the flex of his muscles. The hot ridge of his arousal was like a brand nestled at my core. Once again, we had to break apart to breathe.

Even though I wanted him to be air for me, I did actually need oxygen. We stared at each other in that dark room, that glimmer of light just enough to see.

"Sweetheart," he rasped. "Tell me what you want."

All rational thought had gone up in smoke. I couldn't even consider all the reasons this might not be a good idea or why it might be complicated. *Might* didn't even come close. It *was* complicated. It was beyond reckless for me to do this.

But I just wanted Haven. I wanted this. I took a shaky breath and whispered, "More."

I surprised myself when I reached between us and dragged my palm over his length. His eyes darkened, and his breath hissed through his teeth.

"Elsa," he growled.

He dropped his hands away from the counter, lacing one in my hair as the other curled over my hip.

"Are you sure?" His question lilted up at the end.

With a sharp nod, I bit my lip and rocked my hips against his length, slipping my hand out of the way. He drew in a ragged breath, his eyes still locked to mine.

"I don't know if this is a good idea," he bit out.

"It probably isn't, but I don't care," I whispered, rolling my hips again.

"Let's make one thing clear."

"Okay..."

"If you change your mind at any point, just say so."

I nodded. "The same goes for you."

His low chuckle shimmered over my nerves, already sparking with desire and need.

It was a good thing I was seated because I would have simply melted right to the floor from the heat simmering inside. In a hot second, his lips were on mine again. I let out a whimper when he drew away.

"What?" I protested.

His eyes held mine as he slipped his hand on the hem of my tank top. "Let's get this out of the way, shall we?"

I couldn't move fast enough and almost slowed the process because he was trying to help, and we got tangled. Too many seconds later, he flung my tank top to the floor.

I let out a sigh when he stepped a little closer, and our bare skin met. My nipples were puckered tight, achy for him. He slid one of his hands down my side, his thumb brushing over the side of my breast. My pussy clenched as I gasped, arching into him.

He cupped both breasts, his eyes on mine the whole time as he teased his thumbs over my nipples. I bit my lip, trying to contain the urge to beg.

"Tell me what you want," he repeated in a low rasp.

I felt his words down to my very toes. My toes curled, gasping. I was so overcome with sensation and need, I couldn't even say what I wanted because I wanted *everything*.

As he teased my nipples, he gave me a lingering kiss. Our mouths were open, our tongues tangling, and he drew away, nipping my bottom lip, drawing it out slightly before letting it pop.

More hot, open-mouthed kisses pressed against my neck, trailing down in a lazy blaze of fire. Who knew my collarbone was an erogenous zone? I didn't until his lips teased over it, followed by hot kisses down between my breasts.

My hips rocked into his arousal, and I was crying out, begging. Finally, his lips closed over a nipple, and I almost came from the burst of sensation, the wet suction sizzling like electricity. I felt rushed and needy.

I curled my legs around his hips and hooked my feet around his calves, rocking against him, chasing my release, until he lifted his head. "Elsa, sweetheart, slow down. I want this to be good for you."

I stared at him. I didn't even know what to say, so I sucked in air. His palm smoothed over the curve of my belly. He stepped back slightly as he cupped his hand over my mound, his fingertips pressing against the wet cotton between my thighs.

"One thing at a time," he murmured.

I took a breath, trying to contain the sensation. I was teetering on the edge of a climax already.

"We can make it even better if we take it slow."

"Oh my God!" I finally burst out. "You're going to kill me."

He stepped back with a low chuckle, and I felt bereft, crying out, my breath heaving in protest.

"Just a second..." He slid my hips a little closer to the edge of the counter, curling his fingers over the stretchy cotton of my shorts. He lifted me as he slid them over my hips and down my legs, and I kicked them free. I literally felt his eyes on my sex when he looked down.

My knees had fallen open again, and my pussy was throbbing. I could feel the slick moisture there.

"Oh, sweetheart," he murmured as he teased his fingers into my wet folds.

A few seconds later, he lifted his fingers to his mouth, his eyes on me as he sucked my arousal off. My breath came in sharp pants. My mouth fell open when he dipped his fingers down into me, sinking two inside.

My hips rocked instantly. I was beyond shame, beyond anything other than just wanting this so badly. He pumped his fingers a few times before leaning down and bringing his mouth to my sex.

My hands scrambled to hold the counter. He pumped his fingers in and out, fucking me with them as he circled his tongue around my clit. I was lost as I chased my release. I didn't even know how fast it happened, but it hit me abruptly when he gave the slightest suction over my clit.

The sensation burst through me, his name practically a prayer on my lips. He buried his fingers once more as I trembled. He slowly straightened, and his eyes locked with mine again. It was almost overwhelming how direct he was with eye contact, and I couldn't look away.

I needed more. I needed him inside me. *Now.*

He stepped back. For a moment, I was confused, and then I realized he was getting a condom as he strode into the bathroom. A burning hot moment later, he tore it open and smoothed it on, protecting us both.

"Are you sure?" he asked.

I nodded, my legs still splayed open as he curled his hand around his length, notching his thick cock at my entrance. "Last chance," he said.

"More," I gasped.

Haven filled me in increments until he was seated deeply, and I could hardly breathe, almost climaxing again from the full, delicious stretch of having all of him inside me. He slid his hand around, nudging my hips forward with his palm on my bottom. The friction was incredible. With my legs dangling, my clit was pressing against him right where we were joined.

"Do you want more?"

"Please..." That was all I could say.

Chapter Sixteen

HAVEN

Please...

At Elsa's raspy whispered demand, the crescendo of need pounding through me increased. Staring into her gaze, I sucked in a breath, marshaling my discipline.

On the heels of another breath, I dropped my forehead to hers, and my whisper formed against her lips. "As you wish." Her hips rocked toward me as I filled her again, savoring the clench of her around me. "Elsa," I bit out.

This entire encounter had spun out. The frayed thread of my control was on the verge of snapping. Her palms slid up my back, and she whispered, "More..."

I drew back and filled her once again. She was silky soft, hot, and wet. My release was already threatening, sizzling like lightning down my spine. I pumped into her again and again. She met me, her hips rocking into my thrusts.

Lifting my head, I whispered, "Elsa, look at me."

She dragged her eyes open, and I stayed locked in the blur of her gaze. I reached between us, teasing my fingers over her plump clit. I felt her calves tighten where they curled around the backs of my thighs. Her eyes went wide as her teeth sank into her bottom lip, and her pussy clamped tight.

Her rippling core snapped that frayed thread as my own release struck me with a fiery jolt when I surged into her one more time. I savored my name on her lips and the way she threw her head back.

The feel of her ruched nipples as she arched against my chest nearly brought me to my knees. My hand slapped onto the counter, and I clung to the edge of it, spent.

I leaned into her as she went soft, tucking her head into the curve of my shoulder. With one hand braced on the counter, I slid the other up her back, my fingers lacing into her hair to cradle her against me. The intimacy and raw, exposed feeling should have frightened me. Yet it didn't.

At this moment, I felt better than I ever had. I felt as if Elsa held all of me, keeping me safe. I didn't know how long we stayed like that, with me buried inside her and us holding each other close.

Her palm rested between my shoulder blades. I could feel the rhythm of her heart beating against mine, where she was pressed to the front of me. Our breathing gradually slowed, and my awareness flickered through the haze.

For a split second, I was almost shocked at how I felt. A jolt of fear slammed into my heart, but I kicked it away. This—Elsa, holding her, all of it—felt too good to let anything get in the way. Her soft breath gusted across my skin, and I loved the feeling of it.

My lips curled in a smile when I felt the motion of her lips on my skin, yet one more sensation to catalog along with the rest.

"Well then, that was..."

When she paused, I pondered how it felt and startled myself when I spoke it aloud. "Incredible."

She lifted her head, and I dragged my eyes open to meet hers. She blinked before a smile broke across her face—slow, soft, a ray of sunshine cast through the windows into my heart.

"Yes, incredible," she whispered.

Uncertainty immediately followed that ray of sunshine flickering in her gaze. "I don't usually do that." Her words tumbled out in a rush.

I was flummoxed and eyed her with confusion.

"This." She gestured with her hand vaguely in the air. "Start kissing someone, and then have crazy hot sex on the..." She looked around, taking in the space. "Kitchen counter."

"I don't either, but it's not like we haven't known each other for years," I pointed out.

"I just don't want you to think..." She stopped and bit her lip.

"Think what? I think you're amazing, Elsa. And I think we both needed that."

"What now?" she asked.

My heart gave a tricky twist at Elsa's question. I didn't know what was sensible.

We'd blown far past sensible when I first kissed her. But all I knew, what was guiding me, was what I wanted, which was not to untangle myself from Elsa. I was ready to sign up for *all* the complications. I didn't care about any of them. "What do *you* want to do now?"

She tipped her head to the side, tracing a fingertip along my collarbone. The gesture, kind of sweet, was like the lick of a flame on my skin.

"I don't know. We could watch a movie." She giggled. "I guess that's my way of saying, it feels weird to go back into my bedroom alone and have you on the other side of that wall."

My entire being rebelled against that idea. "Does it feel better if we go back to sleep together?"

She nodded instantly. "Yes."

"Sounds like a plan."

I gave her a lingering kiss, and we disentangled ourselves. After we both tidied up in the bathroom, Elsa stood bashfully outside the side-by-side doors of our bedrooms. "Where do you want to sleep?"

I stopped in front of her, trailing my thumb along the side of her jaw as I cupped her chin and gave her a lingering kiss. "With you. I think you have the better bed."

She leaned her head back to peer up. "You gave me the better bed?" Her eyes went wide.

I chuckled. "I stayed where I did when we stayed here after the fire."

"Who stayed in my room?"

"I think it was Jude, but I'm not sure."

She giggled again and tugged me into her bedroom. This shouldn't have felt so easy, but it did. Being with Elsa *was* easy.

When she fell asleep curled against me, my arm around her with her head resting in the curve of my shoulder, I pondered how right this felt, and how I'd promised myself so many things in the aftermath of the fire.

One of them, remembering to keep what mattered. Elsa mattered. As much as my skeptical mind, my busy life, and so many other things could persuade me this was a bad idea, right now, I just wanted to sleep with Elsa held close. So I did.

ELSA

I tipped my head to the side, studying the barn doors. Jude and Haven had propped the old sign against the side of the barn. Years back, someone had carved it for their grandparents when they first built this place. It was stunning to me how someone could take driftwood gathered from the shore and carve it into this beautiful image of a waterfall.

"Are you sure you want me to paint it?" I asked doubtfully.

When I glanced toward the brothers, Haven stood there casually with his thumb hooked in a belt loop. And, damn, if that man wasn't the definition of a rugged firefighter outdoorsman. He wore a faded denim shirt open over a T-shirt. A strip of his tanned skin was visible where the waistband of his battered pair of jeans tugged down a smidge from the pull on the belt loop.

I doubted the purpose of the T-shirt was meant to be sexy, but on him, it outlined his muscular chest, and his broad shoulders filled it out. The soft-worn fabric invited me to tease my fingers over it.

Jude cleared his throat, and I ripped my eyes away from Haven.

"How ya doing there, Elsa?" Jude teased, a sly glint in his eye.

"I'm fine." My cheeks were burning up, but I was far enough away that I convinced myself Jude couldn't tell.

"Of course, we want it painted," Jude added. "The driftwood is beautiful, but you can't really tell what it's supposed to be."

"It was painted before," Haven added.

When I briefly flicked my gaze to his, the heat in his eyes practically crackled in the air between us.

I cleared my throat. "Okay, tell me what you want."

"We trust your artistic judgment," Jude said, his gaze sober enough that I was pretty sure he was serious.

"Um, okay then. I'll see what I can do."

"Dolly!" At the sound of the goat's name, I glanced over to see Tommy chasing her in the pasture nearby.

A giggle slipped out, and Jude grinned. "All right, you do this. We gotta go help at the rescue program. You coming, Haven?" Jude asked as he began walking away.

Haven stayed in place for a few beats. He shook his head briefly, almost to himself, before tearing his eyes from mine. As they walked away, Haven glanced over his shoulder, and my belly flipped. I was smiling like a goofy, lovestruck girl as I appreciated the view while he walked away.

"Man, oh man," I said to myself, waving a hand to cool my cheeks.

"They *are* handsome boys," a voice said.

I yelped, my palm flying to my chest as I spun around to see Maggie approaching. My cheeks were on fire all over again. I pressed my lips together, trying to think of what to say, and Maggie stopped, her smile warm as she studied me.

"Oh, don't worry. I know you're only crushing on Haven, and he's crushing on you, so I'm all for it. He's in a better mood with you here."

"He is?" My voice lilted up.

She nodded. "He is. How's your mom, by the way?"

"I think she's good. We talk every week. She knows how much I missed Alaska, but..." I paused, gathering my thoughts. "She says she doesn't want to come back to stay."

"Well, your mom did the off-the-grid lifestyle because of your dad. Alaska's kind of a magnet for that, but it's not too enjoyable if it's hardcore." Maggie shook her head a little. "The sad part is, most people in Alaska are self-sufficient, but there's a subset of people where it gets weird. I imagine that taints your mom's memories of this place."

I burst out laughing. "That's one way to put it." I shrugged. "I'm hoping I can persuade her to visit soon, but I don't think she'll ever want to live here, though."

"I understand. You make sure she knows she's always welcome at Heartfire Falls. We're looking fancy these days. She might love it here." Maggie's smile was encouraging.

"She might."

"Honey, I'm glad you're here." Maggie's eyes shone with tears when she reached for my hands and squeezed them.

"I'm glad to be here too. Are you okay?"

She rolled her eyes as she released my hands. "I'm fine, honey. You coming back is like a burst of sunlight in our world. We needed this. I've been so caught up in"—she circled her hand in the air— "the wildfire that burned through here, the world, rebuilding, all this. It's just nice to have somebody here with us who knows what we've been through, but it's different. It's fresh."

"I'm really grateful to be here. Thank you for being so welcoming."

She patted me on the shoulder. "Use your imagination when you're painting that sign. That's what they said."

"You all have a lot of faith in me," I said dryly.

She grinned. "We do."

I spent the afternoon carefully painting the driftwood sign. When I was done, I cleaned up in the utility sink inside the barn before returning outside, hands on my hips as I studied the finished product.

"It looks amazing." Haven's voice came from behind me, its low rumble sending a shiver of heat through me and goose bumps rising on my skin.

I spun around to find him approaching. "You think?" I was nervous because I wasn't an artist. I just liked to have fun with paint sometimes. All this to say, I was satisfied with the result. I just hoped the Silver family would love it.

"I know it looks amazing," Haven said as he stopped in front of me. His presence this close was like a force field, his strength and heat vibrating around me.

For a split second, I thought he was going to kiss me. His blue eyes flashed and heat pooled in my belly. I swallowed as I stared up at him.

"Thank you for doing this," he said.

My mind had gone blank, and I didn't even know what he was thanking me for. The haze in my brain was cleared with another voice.

"Whoa!" Tommy exclaimed. "It's a waterfall!"

Haven and I turned together to see Tommy approaching with two goats following.

"Do you like it?" I asked.

Tommy stopped, clasping his hands together in front of him, appearing quite serious. "Yes," he announced with a nod. "You did that?"

"I did. It was kind of fun. I'm glad you like it."

He grinned. "Wow, it feels like this is really happening."

"What's really happening?" Haven asked as he ruffled Tommy's hair affectionately.

"We're opening, right? Soon?" Tommy rubbed his hands together in excitement. "Do I get to lead some of the hikes?"

The love in Haven's eyes as he looked down at Tommy turned my heart soft.

"You can come with us sometimes, but you'll be at school most of the time," Haven pointed out.

"What about summer?" Tommy threw his hands up.

"That's when you can come with us," Haven added.

Tommy looked a little let down at this. He scrunched his nose as he peered up at his father. "Didn't you guys lead hikes when you were kids?"

"Our dad was always there, or our granddad, so that's how you'll do it."

"So I can go in front?"

Haven's lips curled in a soft smile. "Yes, you can go in front. When you're not at school."

Tommy beamed before lifting his gaze back up to the waterfall sign. I'd painted it blue mixed with shades of gold and a little orange— just how it looked when the sun struck the water as it fell. Hence its official name, Heartfire Falls Resort.

"Thanks, Elsa," Tommy said.

I glanced down at him. "For what?"

He rolled his eyes, throwing his hands out toward the sign. "That. It's pretty, and it's fun for me." Without another word, Tommy spun around. "I have to take the goats back." With a wave, he was off.

"Be on time for dinner," Haven called to his departing back.

Chapter Eighteen

ELSA

"He's a really good kid," I said when Haven glanced back toward me.

"He is."

"How old was he when this place burned down?"

Haven said, "He was born while Bree was in the hospital after the fire."

He rarely spoke much about the fire and Bree dying, but whenever it came up, you could see the pain shoved deep in his heart and its brief flare in his eyes.

"I'm so, so sorry, Haven."

He stuffed his hands in his pockets. "We all are."

I wanted to say more, but it didn't feel like the time.

He glanced toward the sign. "It really does look good. Without you here"—he shrugged— "we would have just nailed it up and hoped for the best."

"I'm sure it would have been fine."

He tipped his head to the side, studying me, and I started to feel hot all over. "What?" I pressed, shifting on my feet.

"You know, you could just take a thank you or a compliment. Wouldn't hurt you."

I felt the blush rising into my cheeks, shrugging as I scuffed the toe of my worn cowboy boot in the gravel. "I'm not that good at that."

He pressed his tongue into his cheek as a smile slowly stretched across his face. "Oh, I didn't notice," he deadpanned.

This time, I kicked the toe of my boot against his. "Hey, Mr. Grumpy, you ignore compliments and thank-yous too."

He chuckled. "Fair point."

I was about to ask what had changed him from the previously easy-going guy I'd known in passing when we were younger into this, but I knew the answer. Losing his dad, and then the fire, and his sister. Those events had been one blow after another, crowded together.

He had shouldered all of it as the oldest of the brothers. While it was clear they were all taking care of Tommy, he was the one who made it official because somebody had to make it official.

"What?" he prompted.

I took a quick breath. "You're a good man, Haven Silver."

"Hmm." That was all he had to say to that. "You'll be at dinner?"

I nodded. "Your mom seems to like it when I'm there."

He chuckled. "She loves having you here."

His gaze darkened as he studied me. "And after?"

"After what?"

"Where will you be after dinner?"

I was instantly flustered as I gestured vaguely in the direction of the barn. "There?" I finally said.

"Good."

"What does that mean?" I called after his retreating back.

———

That night, dinner was delicious, and I did my best to ignore how I got flustered *every time* I looked at Haven. Why did he have to be so handsome? It was incredibly unfair and distracting. He came walking in all brawny and strong with that long stride and sat down directly across from me. It was all I could do to keep from wiggling in my seat under the burn of his gaze.

Tommy talked nonstop tonight, conversation leaping from one

topic to the next. Afterward, I helped Maggie clean up. I heard the rumble of the brothers' voices as they discussed scheduling some things.

"Thank you for putting that ad up," Maggie said as I tucked the last dish into the dishwasher.

"Of course. I'm sure you'll get some good applicants."

"We already have some, and I'm hoping you'll sit in on the interviews."

"Oh really?" I glanced toward her.

"Please. I need someone other than me to screen for tech skills to handle this stuff."

"You schedule them, and I'll be there. I start work Monday, so if it's after Monday, we'll have to do them after four thirty."

"No problem. The sign looks beautiful," she added as I began to turn away.

"It was no trouble. I'm glad you like it." My mind spun to Haven, pointing out I didn't take compliments well, and I forced myself to just accept the compliment.

Just then, Tommy came in to ask Maggie for help with his math homework, and I decided to make my way out. I was hoping to get back to the house and be changed before Haven showed up.

It wasn't like I needed to hide from him, but I didn't know what I was supposed to do. Last night felt monumental, but what were we now?

Chapter Nineteen

HAVEN

Anticipation buzzed in my system as I crested the top stair into the apartment above the barn. When I walked in, Elsa was at the kitchen counter, rinsing something in the sink. She didn't appear to have heard me. Her hair was pulled up in a messy bun, and she'd changed out of whatever she'd been wearing earlier. Honestly, I didn't even remember.

She could wear a potato sack, and I wouldn't notice. But now, I *did* notice because she wore these swingy soft pants that she probably didn't know outlined her plump bottom perfectly.

I slipped out of my boots and walked straight across the room, stopping behind her and resting my hands on the counter on either side of her hips. She squeaked, glancing over her shoulder.

"Hi," I murmured.

The pink wash on her cheeks thickened my arousal. I stepped a little closer because I wanted to feel the soft curves of her bottom against me. Her breath sucked in, and her teeth snagged her bottom lip.

"Haven," she whispered.

Her breath drawing in sharply sizzled through me, and I stepped a little closer.

"We, uh, didn't talk about this," she added.

I was admittedly a little disappointed when she turned around because I loved the feel of her bottom, but then I discovered she wasn't wearing a bra because her nipples were pressing through the thin fabric of her T-shirt.

"Talk about what?"

"You know." She circled her hand between us.

She held a towel in her other hand, and I reached for it, tossing it on the counter beside us. "About how hot last night was?" I prompted.

She cleared her throat, the flush on her cheeks deepening. "Um, yeah, that."

"Okay, let's talk now."

She let out a flustered sigh. "Haven, you're standing so close I can't think."

"Do you want me to go away?"

Another flustered sigh. "No, I mean…"

"Look, Elsa." I decided to be blunt. "It's *really* good with us. Or at least it is for me." She nodded. "Does that mean you agree with how good it is?"

She rolled her eyes. "Obviously. And I like you, but it's complicated."

"I like you too. What's complicated?"

"I'm staying here." She sighed again.

"I'll be even blunter. Everything feels better with you here. We could just let this roll and see how that goes," I offered.

"I don't have anywhere to go if you kick me out," she pointed out.

I forced myself to stay focused. "I'm not going to kick you out. I promise."

Distracted by the weight of her teeth denting her luscious bottom lip, I tried to rein in my need for her. Fuck me. I couldn't help my body's reflexive response when I rocked my hips into the cradle of hers. I was gratified when she let out a whimpery sigh.

I realized she had a point, though. My default setting was good guy. It was a fact that between my dad dying, the fire, and Bree dying, the guy in me who used to be nicer and more easygoing had mostly been overtaken by, as my mom said, a cranky grump.

But I wasn't an asshole. "I don't mean to pressure you." I lifted my hands away and started to take a step back.

Elsa reached out, hooking her finger around my belt loop and pulling me back. "You're not pressuring me. Obviously, it's good between us. Let's just agree that if things get complicated, we'll put a stop to it."

Relief shafted through me. "Deal."

Her gaze turned sultry as she dragged her palm over the ridge of my arousal. "Where were we?"

My chuckle was followed by a groan when she deftly unbuttoned my jeans and slipped her sweet hand into my boxers, instantly curling around my length. Elsa's eyes were dark, and I could barely catch my breath. She teased my arousal just as I started to speak, and my words stalled.

She shoved my jeans down around my hips just enough for my cock to spring free. She slid her thumb over the pre-cum already rolling out of the tip. "Elsa," I bit out.

Her tongue darted out, swiping across her bottom lip, the sight of that sending another jolt of blood to my aching arousal.

"Elsa, what?" Her teasing tone was sultry, and I couldn't even think over the rush of need coursing through me.

She leaned forward, her tongue swirling around the tip of my cock before she sucked me in. Lacing my fingers in her hair with one hand, I slapped my other against the counter as I braced myself for the onslaught of pleasurable torture.

She drew back, tipping her head to the side. As I looked down at her, she released me with a pop. "Do you want more?"

"Fuck, Elsa," I groaned.

"That's not an answer," she teased.

I clenched my teeth, and she sucked me in again. Holy hell. She drove me to near distraction with her palm curled around my length, sliding up and down with the motion of her mouth. She released me, her tongue teasing along the underside before swirling around my crown again and once more sucking me in.

My fingers gripped her hair, my other palm flexing on the counter, sliding to grip the edge. I didn't know how much I could take until, yet again, she sucked just hard enough, and my release whipped through me. She leaned back as it spurted over her hand.

I held on to that counter and her hair to keep my knees from buckling. My breath was coming in heaves. I eased my hold on her hair when she slowly straightened. A moment later, she rinsed her hands in the sink.

I opened my mouth to say something, but she took care of me too, tidying me up. Her lips curled at the corners, her smile satisfied and sweet when she bit her lip. The glint in her eyes was playful.

Those few moments had given me enough strength to collect myself. I gulped in a deep breath.

"Your turn," I said, pushing away from the counter and reaching for her hand.

Her eyes widened slightly, and I chuckled. "It's never a one-way street with me, sweetheart."

Chapter Twenty

ELSA

Haven's eyes burned into me. I felt his gaze on my skin as it swept up and down. My nipples perked up, and heat pooled in my belly. I had to press my thighs together.

"Where are we going?" I rasped as he turned and tugged me to follow.

"Somewhere horizontal," he said flatly.

I giggled as he tugged me into my room since we'd established this room had the better bed. Once we got into the bedroom, Haven turned to face me. "You're wearing too many clothes," he pointed out. "Let's remedy that."

He swiftly tugged my shirt over my head. At the feel of the calloused surface of his palms cupping my breasts, I had to bite my lip to keep from whimpering too loudly. His thumbs brushed over my nipples before he dipped his head and sucked one into his mouth.

I cried out, my knees buckling. One arm banded around my waist as he held me steady before lifting his head and bringing his mouth to mine. Haven's kisses were enough to make me want to pledge my body to him forever. The way he commanded my mouth was just perfect— deep sweeps of his tongue and open, hot, messy kisses—and all the while, I was melting inside. I could feel my slick arousal between my thighs and shifted on my feet.

He broke away, his teeth nipping at my bottom lip as his eyes burned into mine again.

"Now, you're wearing too many clothes," I gasped.

His low chuckle sent goose bumps rising on my skin. When he stepped back, I instantly missed his strong presence and the way it surrounded me.

The next few moments were a blur. I tossed my shirt and bra to the floor and fumbled to remove my jeans. His clothes fell in a rumple along with mine on the floor. He stretched me out on the bed as I trembled with arousal. There was something about him, the way he looked at me, the way I felt as if he savored every inch of me, that nearly undid me.

"Elsa," he groaned as one of his big palms caressed down my side, his thumb teasing over my nipple briefly before his touch coasted down over my belly, rounding the curve of my hip and down my thighs.

I'd never been a skinny girl, definitely wasn't now, but he seemed to love it, squeezing my hip and then my thigh as he made a humming sound of appreciation in his throat. His eyes burned into mine for a beat before he dipped his head, his tongue dragging down the side of my neck. Hot kisses dusted over my belly before he teased my nipples with his mouth.

All the while, I whimpered and arched into his touch. He made his way down my body before hooking his hand under one knee and pressing it to the side.

"Sweet Elsa," he murmured as his fingers teased my dripping wet pussy. "Look at you."

I dragged my eyes open, and I could have sworn I felt the heat of his gaze on my sex. I clenched in response, my hips shifting restlessly on the bed. I'd never felt so exposed to someone. He blew lightly just before he brought his mouth to my sex, and I felt two fingers sliding in. My hips rocked into his touch as he made love to me with his fingers and his mouth. Everything was tightening, spinning inside, the pleasure rising.

I felt the vibration of him saying something against me just before he circled his tongue around my clit. The graze of his teeth sent sensations streaking through me as he pumped his fingers in once more.

"Come for me, sweetheart. I know you're almost there."

Apparently, I could come on his command because I did just that. The tightening reached an almost unbearable point before snapping. I cried out, shuddering all over as I arched into him. He stayed with me as pleasure broke in wave after wave.

I finally sagged in relief. He slowly stretched up beside me, pressing kisses, open and hot, on my neck. When I dragged my eyes open, he gave me a lazy kiss, and I could taste myself on his mouth. My body was still trembling from the aftershocks of my climax.

Haven dusted a kiss on the curve where my shoulder met my neck, and I savored the feel of his stubbled cheek. "How are you doing?" he asked.

A giggle slipped out at that. "How am I doing?" I was practically slurring from pleasure.

He lifted his head, a sly gleam in his eyes. "I guess I'm wondering if you're as useless as I was after what you did to me out there in the kitchen."

I felt almost boneless, completely sated as I rested on the bed. "Definitely useless. If there was an emergency, I don't even know if I could move."

Another kiss, this one in the valley between my breasts. The heat of it radiated through me. Even though I was pretty useless, my nipples perked up, and my pussy clenched.

"We can call it a night," he murmured.

"Oh, no." I rolled my head back and forth on the pillow. "I need more."

His grin sent my belly into a swoop. He rolled over to get off the bed. "I didn't mean getting off the bed more," I protested.

"Condom," he tossed over his shoulder.

Part of me wanted to call out that it wasn't necessary, but this was fresh, so I held my silence. A moment later, he was back and rolling a condom on. I looked up as one of his knees landed between my thighs.

Sweet hell. Haven Silver was one rugged, sexy man. All muscled, but not in a workout way. He had a dusting of dark hair on his chest and a few scars here and there. I wanted to trace my fingers over them and ask him how he got every single one. But before I could even form another thought, his weight stretched out over me.

I instantly made room for his hips in the cradle of mine. My breath sucked in when he notched his thick crown at my entrance.

"Are you still ready for more?" His subtle tease was in contrast to his gaze, which was intense and serious.

"I always want more with you," I whispered.

He shifted carefully, reaching for both of my hands and stretching them out above my head. On the heels of a breath, he slowly filled me, seating himself deeply. I let out something between a moan and a whimper and curled my legs around his hips.

When his eyes locked with mine, I couldn't look away. He held still, and I felt myself pulsing around him. The next span of time was a blur.

I was lost in his gaze and the sensation of him surging into me again and again to the soundtrack of our ragged breathing. Both of us were chasing another release. Everything was a tangle of sensation.

The subtle prickle of his hair on my breasts. The way his muscles flexed with his motion. His hands gripping mine. Through it all, I felt completely vulnerable and split wide open, but safe.

He adjusted the angle of his hips and reached between us with one of his hands, teasing over my hypersensitive nub. Yet again, pleasure exploded. This time, my orgasm was deeper and slower, a vibration under the surface that rocked me all the way through. I barely recognized the sound of me calling his name and holding on tight as my name came in a ragged breath on his lips.

Moments later, he rolled us over, and I rested against him. It felt as if I'd been through a storm, my body exhausted from it. My head curled on his chest, and I listened to his heart thumping and gradually slowing.

His fingers sifted through my hair before his palm slid down my back to cup my bottom. There was something so purely masculine about everything he did. His touch was casual and easy.

"I could stay here forever." As soon as I said those words, I wanted to snatch them back.

Because that seemed like, well, *a lot* to say at this stage in whatever this was.

"I could too," he replied.

I lifted my head, resting my palm on his chest and my chin atop that.

"Is this when I should find a way to leave?" His voice rumbled under my hand.

"Where would you go?" His lips quirked a little at the corners, and my belly shimmied again.

So help me God, my body just wouldn't quit when it came to this man.

"To my bedroom," he replied.

I rolled my eyes. "No."

I loved that he chuckled. Before I knew it, we were laughing together. I felt ridiculous and giddy when my laugh finally slowed down.

I took a quick breath. "Haven Silver."

"Right here," he returned, waggling his brows. "It's my name, don't you forget it."

"As if," I teased.

Suddenly, his gaze sobered, and he tipped his head to the side. "How are you doing?"

"What do you mean?"

He shrugged, his shoulder moving underneath mine where it rested against his. "You were worried about complications."

"Well, it's day two, and we *are* dealing with complications. I think your mom's on to us."

His lips teased in another smile. "She's observant. I haven't said a word to her, but I have no doubt she's noticed I can't keep my eyes off you."

"You can't?" I squeaked.

"Elsa, honey, you're adorable, you're funny, and I'm really glad you're here."

Although my doubts were kicking up a storm in my mind, I ignored them. "I'm glad I'm here too."

By some freaking miracle, we didn't dwell on that. We lazed in bed, talking about nothing and everything. I filled him in on scheduling interviews with his mom, and he gave me a few pointers about the kind of personality that would fit to work with her.

"She's easy-going most of the time. But underneath that is a stubborn woman who likes things done a certain way. She isn't that tech-savvy, so this will take some letting go on her part," he explained.

"Okay, so basically, I have to find someone who can baby her without her noticing it."

He grinned. "You got it."

He told me more about how long they'd been working on rebuilding the resort because it took so long to deal with the insurance. Then he tugged me into the shower, and we fell asleep together. Again.

———

As the days rolled by, I decided to ignore all the potential problems the complications could create. I enjoyed dinners with the family. I helped finish painting the guest rooms for the resort opening. Tommy took me on a tour of the rescue program.

I even got up the nerve to invite my mom for a visit.

Me: *Maggie says you can come visit.*

Mom: *I know I can, sweetie, and I probably will. But not just yet.*

After a few days, I walked back over to our property, studying the old foundation and remembering my dad. He meant well, but he might still be here if he hadn't been so committed to being independent and eschewing any help.

"We'll help you build." Haven's voice reached me, carried on the gusts of the wind that blew toward me.

I turned and cast a smile over my shoulder. "I know you will. I'll figure it out. First, I have to start work."

It was a chilly late summer afternoon. When I shivered a little with another gust of wind, Haven stepped closer and reached for my hands, tucking them into his pockets with his.

The gesture was so sweet, my heart flipped in my chest. "If anybody catches you doing that, they'll think you're sweet on me."

His smile was slow and devastating for my heart, and like gas on a fire for my hormones. "I *am* sweet on you."

I swear, I blushed from head to toe. He dipped his head and gave me a lingering kiss, and it washed over me. I couldn't help but just feel good.

"Mom said you walked out here, so I came to find you. She was hoping you could check in with her before the interview," Haven said when he lifted his head.

"Oh, that's right. I should go."

"You're not late," he said as I started to move. "Half an hour."

Then he kissed me again, and I forgot everything else. I didn't know how long it lasted, but I realized I could stand outside in the fresh air, with the fireweed ablaze in the background and the wind blowing, with my hands tucked into Haven's pockets and him kissing me, for *all* the days of my life.

No matter what happened, I knew this was a memory I would keep.

That was something my mom talked about a lot after my dad died —what we kept in our hearts.

I was also starting to worry that I wasn't cut out for casual. Not that Haven promised this would be casual. But a tiny corner of my mind and heart was more than a little worried.

Chapter Twenty-One

HAVEN

"Where's Elsa?" Jude asked as he approached me, where I was eyeing the finish trim I was putting on the desk in one of the offices.

"Today's her first day at work," I replied.

Jude tapped his fingers to the side of his head. "That's right. Totally spaced it." He plunked down in the chair across from me. "We're almost there."

"I know," I replied with a glance up.

"Really glad Elsa's here."

"Yeah." I kept my tone vague. I was more than glad she was here, but I didn't think Jude shared my specific reasons.

"Yeah, she knocked out the painting quick, and that sign out on the barn looks amazing. I think we're ready to roll. You think Lincoln will come back soon?" he asked next.

Lincoln. Our missing brother.

I tapped the last nail on the trim and straightened as I set down the hammer. "I don't know. He's with a hotshot crew up in Fairbanks. We all rotate out."

"He doesn't rotate out. He's gone most of the time," Jude pointed out.

"I know." I bit back the sigh rattling in my chest.

Lincoln had taken Bree's death a little harder than the rest of us. It seemed to have been a body blow for him, where he pulled away instead of turning toward us. We were all worried, but most of our worry was left unspoken because I guess we all figured he just needed time.

"Mom thinks you're in love with Elsa," Jude said next.

I almost choked on the swallow of water I'd just taken from a bottle. I lowered it and dragged my sleeve across my chin. "Excuse me?" I said between coughs.

Jude waggled his brows. "I'm inclined to agree with Mom on this."

"Jude..." I warned.

"Look, I guess we're all worried about each other. But phew." He let out a low whistle. "You could win a medal for being a cranky ass, but since Elsa's been here, you've lightened up a little. I think she's good for you."

I shifted my shoulders as I sank my hips into the chair by the desk, letting out a heavy sigh and running a hand through my hair. I knew damn well I'd been more irritable since Bree died. But well, our whole family had been a mess. I wasn't short on reasons to be stressed out.

"Jude, Dad died, then within a year, the whole place burned down and Bree died. It's been stressful."

"Well, your mood's been a hell of a lot better since Elsa's been around. So don't be a dumbass." At that, he tapped his fingers on the desk and stood to leave.

It was startling how quickly I adjusted to Elsa being here all day, every day. I didn't want to think about missing her when she started her job, but I did. That worry feathered along my thoughts until the day she actually did, and I carried a piercing ache in my heart. She was just at work, but that was how bad I had it for her.

As I walked through my days, which were always busy, I missed the light, teasing sound of her voice, her asking my brothers for their opinions on the paint and so on. But I kicked those thoughts away. Until Cole pointed out, "Man, I forgot how grumpy you could be."

"What are you talking about?" I asked.

He rolled his eyes. "Elsa's not here full-time now, and you've reverted."

"Reverted?"

Jude chuckled as he plunked down in a chair at the kitchen table. "Yep. We're going to have to adjust."

I rolled my eyes. "Cut the shit."

"Why? You like Elsa. Just admit it," Jude said.

"We *all* like her," I pointed out.

"She's the best thing that's happened to you since—" Cole began.

"Since when?" Tommy asked as he entered the kitchen.

For a moment, the mood turned serious, but it passed quickly, because we all knew this drill. We didn't dwell on Bree's death, especially not around Tommy.

"Your dad's just cranky sometimes," Jude pointed out lightly.

"I know, but he's been in a better mood lately. I think it's Elsa," Tommy said with a somber nod as though he was a freaking genius about relationships.

Asher chuckled as he walked into the kitchen. "From the mouths of babes. You are smart, my man." He clapped Tommy on the shoulder.

"And I won the spelling bee at school today!" Tommy announced.

"You did? That's awesome!" I exclaimed.

"Yes, I've been studying. That's what you told me to do, and Elsa tested me the other day," Tommy explained.

"She did?" I prompted, wondering what else I'd missed.

"Yeah, she was painting, and I was doing my homework, and I needed someone to test me, so she put the notebook on the floor while she kept painting, and we ran through a whole bunch of words. She's a good speller." Tommy nodded vigorously at that.

My brain went where it wasn't supposed to. Elsa was good at a lot of things, including some that made my body very happy. I didn't think about how impatient I was to get to tonight when I would have some time with just her.

I forced my mind off that train of thought. "Well, rock on. Since you won your spelling bee, what do you want for dinner?"

"I don't know. What's Grandma making?"

"Well, you know it'll be whatever you want. We have something to celebrate," I said.

Tommy considered this seriously. "I'm gonna go ask her what my options are."

We all high-fived him before he left the room, and then I dragged the laptop over in front of me. "All right, we gotta do some planning, guys. Mom says she and Elsa have hired somebody who's starting next week. They'll sort out the reservations and so on, and in the meantime, we need to take a look at the budget."

"Oh, the fucking budget." Jude sighed and ran a hand through his hair. "We need an accountant."

"Once we're up and running and bringing money in, we can hire one," I pointed out. "In the meantime, well, it's me."

"I know. And you're stingy," Cole chimed in.

"I'm not stingy. I just want us to make this work. We haven't had any income from this place since it burned down. Thank God we're all trained firefighters because that's what we used to get by. But it's also part of why building this place has taken us so long. Separate from the time it took to get the insurance money for the construction, let's just look at everything so we know where we're at."

"I mean, the way it worked before, Dad did firefighting, right?" Asher asked.

"Oh yeah, he did, but the resort was also a smaller operation. We've got more rooms now, and even Dad hired out for help," Cole said.

"As long as four of us are here, two of us can rotate out with the hotshot crew when they need someone extra," I explained.

"How many people do we have on the waitlist?" Jude prompted.

I clicked on the screen where our mom had been keeping a list and let out a low whistle. "Over forty."

"Holy shit," Asher breathed.

"Yeah, Mom booked twenty of them already for three weeks from now," I explained.

"Okay, this is really good news," Jude said, nodding. "And a shit ton of work."

"The rooms are ready to go. Whoever's helping with the computer stuff and the reservations, we'll need their help with supplies because people can come stay, but we need… oh fuck. I'll talk to Mom." I ran a hand through my hair.

"Do we need Lincoln to come back?" Cole asked.

"Nope, we're good for now. "I looked around at my brothers, realizing, not for the first time, that I was the only one of us who had been an adult at the time of the fire. While we'd all grown up here and been a part of the family's business, for them, it had been tagging along after school and during summers.

Bree had been an adult, but she was gone. I'd been the one who helped Dad and had a better sense of the logistics of the business before he passed. I glanced at my brothers. "We've got this. I promise."

Cole leaned back in his chair, nodding to himself. "We do. This was the plan all along."

"Well, it's only been delayed by a whole freakin' year," Jude cut in with a dry chuckle.

"That's construction for ya," I returned. "We're more than ready. We have to be." I only hoped we could convey our confidence into action.

Just then, our mother came in and started reeling off all the things she'd already taken care of as far as supplies for the guests. When Cole started to look worried, she squeezed his shoulder. "We've got this. You boys might be the tough ones and the firefighters, but I ran this business with my parents and then with your dad. I've got it. The only part I don't have to do is trek out in the wilderness to fish or hunt or whatever else." She rolled her eyes. "You've got the fun part, but it stresses me out."

After my brothers departed, I glanced over at my mom. "They want to be more a part of this, Mom."

It was rare for her sorrow to break through, but she swiped at the tears glittering on her eyelashes. "I know they do, and your dad always said I could be kind of bossy. The new employee, her name's Chloe, is starting tomorrow. Between her and Elsa, I feel ready."

"I miss Dad. And Bree." The words slipped out before they'd even fully formed in my thoughts.

"We all do." She took a deep breath. "Life has changed. There isn't a day that goes by when I don't miss your father, and I'm beyond grateful that all of you wanted to be a part of this."

"There was never any question about that, Mom." My voice was low.

She shrugged lightly. "I know, but it's the kind of thing you've got to love to do. And after the fire..." She closed her eyes briefly as she took another breath. "That could have scattered us to the winds. Instead, it seems to have brought us together."

My chest ached thinking about Bree and my dad. I quickly shifted the subject, checking in with her to cross-check her handwritten list with the one Elsa had made for her on the computer. When we were done, I closed the laptop.

She tilted her head to the side. "I like Elsa," she announced. The moment she spoke, I knew this was going somewhere.

"I like Elsa, too. Pretty sure we all like her. She's likable." I kept my tone light, hoping my mom didn't press too much.

My mom bit her lip, pressing them together as if trying to keep from laughing before finally snorting. "She *is* very likable. But I think you like her in more than just a friendly way."

"Okaaaay," I said slowly.

"You be good to her."

"Of course, I'll be good to her, Mom. Aren't you supposed to be protecting me? I'm your son," I pointed out.

She waggled her brows. "Of course, I protect you. But..." She paused. "There's something a little special about Elsa. I think you know what I mean."

My heart squeezed tight because I knew exactly what she meant. There was something more than a *little* special about Elsa.

When Elsa walked into a room, everything felt a little lighter. Her smile itself was sunshine. And it wasn't as if life had been perfect for her. She'd lost her own father, and I knew she grieved him. But her sweet smile, radiant warmth, and that soft uncertainty underneath—as if she wasn't sure she belonged—made me want to give her everything, to unfurl the world for her and ensure she always knew just how special she was.

My voice was gruff when I replied, "I know she's special."

"I know you'll be good to her, and you definitely have been in a better mood since she's been here. But then, I think we kind of all have."

"Elsa has that effect," I said with a chuckle.

"She does. And maybe, just maybe, you could give yourself a chance."

"What do you mean?" I narrowed my eyes.

"You know what I mean." My mother stood from the table, pecked me on the cheek, and gave my shoulder a squeeze before she walked out of the room to leave me to ponder *that* observation.

ELSA

I was covered in sand, and my skin stung from the ocean salt drying on my hands and arms. When I straightened from putting away my gear and looked into Cook Inlet to see a pod of beluga whales swimming through the water, pure joy rose in a cacophony. There were so many reasons I'd wanted to come back to Alaska, but this moment crystallized them.

The wildness, the crisp air, the wind, the ocean, and my dream job. It was my dream because I felt so real when I was in this place with a sense of grounding inside after feeling unmoored during my time away. I smiled as I hefted my backpack onto my shoulder and turned.

Just before I climbed into my car, I took a last look, whispering, "I'll be back," because I would.

Week one at my job felt perfect. Of course, the start involved a lot of administrative details, but I loved my boss. She'd immediately assigned me to three local monitoring projects, lifted her hands, and said, "They're all yours. I know you know what to do, and I know you love this work."

I'd almost burst into happy tears in her office, but I kept it together. On the drive home, I swung by Firehouse Café to grab a coffee. Another thing I loved about Alaska was you could walk into just about any restaurant in rubber boots and sand-covered jeans, and nobody would blink.

That's how it was here. Fancy rubbed shoulders with down-to-earth. The only thing that mattered was what was in your heart.

Janet grinned at me from behind the counter. "I don't see you here that often," I pointed out.

"Well, you haven't been here that often," she returned with a grin. "I hear you're settling in well out at Heartfire Falls."

"Where did you hear that?" I didn't think anybody knew, even if Maggie suspected, that anything had happened between Haven and me. But this was a small town, and gossip traveled through the winding lines of communication as fast as sparks flew into the air when a fire was blazing.

"Maggie. She stops in every week. She told me you helped paint and that the sign looks amazing. I'm coming out for dinner one night this week, so I'll get to see it."

"You are?"

"Yeah, I do that when I can. Maggie and I are old friends."

"Of course you are," I said with a shrug, feeling a little sheepish because that should have been obvious.

"Have you heard from your mom?" Janet asked.

"I call her once or twice a week, and we text often. I'm hoping she'll come, at least for a visit, but..." I let out a sigh.

Janet tipped her head to the side as she studied me. "Her feelings are a little more complicated than yours."

"And painful," I pointed out.

"We all have complicated feelings about the places we grow up." Janet's voice was matter-of-fact.

"I know."

"And it was different for you, honey. Your dad's off-the-grid thing was stressful for a parent, especially when he..." She hesitated. "When he got sick. Most of your childhood, you were a girl with plenty of fun things to do outdoors, so you probably didn't feel the burden of it the way your mom did."

"I know." I *did* know. Maybe I hadn't grasped it at the time, but I'd felt the anxiety emanating from my mother so often. "That's not how they live at the resort, though. They have all the amenities."

Janet's gaze softened. "Give her time." Janet's eyes studied me, taking in my sand-covered boots. "Where have you been today?"

I chuckled. "I started my job, and I was out doing some monitoring on one of the beluga pods in Cook Inlet. I got a little sandy."

"Obviously, you're going to love your job."

"I already love my job."

"Elsa?" a voice called from behind me.

I spun around and studied the woman approaching. "Tiffany?"

"That's me!"

"Oh wow, how are you?"

Tiffany pulled me into a big hug. Since my life was sort of isolated as a kid, I didn't have many friends, but I had some. Tiffany had always been friendly and affectionate. She peppered me with questions, and when she heard I was out at Heartfire Falls, she smiled.

She let out a low whistle. "Those Silver boys are easy on the eyes."

"Do we call them 'those Silver boys'?" I teased.

"Well, around town, we do. They don't firefight full-time, but they help out on the crews every summer." She paused, her gaze sobering. "And then, well, things haven't been easy on that family."

"I know." My breath came out in a gust, just thinking of all they'd been through.

"Sorry to interrupt, girls," Janet said. "I need to take your orders because more customers are coming in behind you."

Tiffany and I quickly ordered. I sat down with her, getting updates on her life and filling her in on mine. The sketch of my life was basic right now, and I avoided mentioning the smokin'-hot nights I'd shared with Haven altogether.

"Oh, wait a second. Your mother-in-law runs the animal program," I said mid-conversation.

Tiffany flashed a smile. "Bingo. That's why I'm so up to speed on those Silver boys. When we kept getting requests for larger animal rescues after the wildfire blew through the outskirts of town, the family let us lease one of their old barns and use part of the property. It's worked out great. Haven's son, Tommy, works there for us in the afternoons. He does the evening feeding, checks on everyone, and so on. Love that family. I'm so glad you landed out there and got such a great job!" She paused, tilting her head to the side. "We do a girls' night thing—dinner and casual cards. It's usually once or twice a month. You should come."

Insecurity reared its head inside because, well, having the dad I did —may his sweet, misguided heart rest in peace—meant I didn't get to do a lot of the typical social activities.

She must've seen the uncertainty in my gaze. "Come on. I promise you'll love it. Give me your number."

Before I knew it, I exchanged numbers with her, and she told me she'd be texting me for the next one. As I drove home, everything felt good about my life. I was downright giddy.

I debated whether I should stop by the barn apartment to shower before dinner, but I decided against it. Maggie liked us to be on time for dinner. The Silver boys, I laughed to myself at that, showed up sometimes with the dusty, dirty clothes of men who worked and lived in the outdoors. They washed their hands, and that was good enough.

I helped Maggie because I happened to be the first one to arrive. I thought maybe this would be good. Haven would take one look at me —my hair a wild mess, my messy bun taken to new levels—and, well, maybe it would cool his ardor. I was starting to worry things were spiraling out of control for us.

It's not going to cool yours, girl, my mind taunted me. I ignored it.

Of course, he sat down across from me again. I was pretty sure he did that just to torture me. When his eyes met mine, I got hot all over. My nipples perked up, pressing against the thin fabric of my T-shirt. I felt his gaze dip down, and when it lifted back to mine, there was a sly gleam there.

Chapter Twenty-Three

ELSA

When Haven walked into the apartment a while later, I ordered my hormones to stand down and my belly to stop feeling all hot and tingly. I'd hustled over here after dinner, if only because I was trying not to behave like a silly girl with a crush and linger near him. He toed his boots off by the door and began walking across the room before stopping a few feet away.

"What?" he asked.

"What do you mean?" I countered.

I knew my cheeks were red because the heat was burning me up inside. Honestly, it wasn't fair. Haven was one of those guys who looked maddeningly hot without even trying. He was the definition of lumbersexual. My God—at the moment, he was wearing jeans so faded and soft that they molded to his muscled thighs as if the fabric itself had a thing for him.

When he lifted his big, strong hand—a hand that had touched all the parts of me, a hand that I knew felt good everywhere—to run it through his hair, his shirt lifted a little at the bottom. That faded navy T-shirt illuminated the blue of his eyes.

I swear, clothes for this man were made just to show him off. His broad shoulders, his lean, muscled chest and back. I mentally shook my thoughts back to my point. His T-shirt hitched up just high enough that I got a teasing peek at his muscled abs. I didn't even know how it was possible, but the heat cranked hotter inside me.

He dropped his hand, and his now mussed hair was even sexier.

"Elsa, you have..." He circled his hand in the air. "I don't know... a look. Are you okay?"

Fair question. I wasn't okay. Not at all. I needed him to slake the need pounding like an impatient fist on a door into my heart and body.

I wanted him naked and buried inside me, but first, I wanted the foreplay because, holy hell, Haven Silver gave good foreplay.

"I'm fine," I squeaked.

I stood by the kitchen counter and backed up as he approached. I could have sworn his eyes darkened, but that had to be all in my head. By the time he stopped in front of me, I could hardly catch my breath, and my pulse had snapped loose from the thin tether restraining it. I questioned if it was possible for me to survive the pace of my heartbeat. Maybe I would just die from it, and then I wouldn't have to deal with a broken heart. Haven was going to ruin me.

"I don't think you're fine." He paused, shaking his head slightly before his lips kicked up in that half grin that sent my belly into a crazy swoop. "To clarify, you are *fine*, but I don't think that's what you mean."

I managed to roll my eyes, and then suddenly, I lost the capacity to play it cool.

"Haven..." My voice had a frayed edge. "I'm worried. This is getting more complicated than I could have imagined when I said this could get complicated."

"Hey, it's okay." His voice was soothing, and my heart felt splayed wide open because, sweet hell, I didn't need this man to try to comfort me. I suddenly wanted to cry.

"I feel really good with you. I like you, and I'm afraid." I blinked, silently praying not to cry.

He stepped closer, lifting a hand to palm my cheek. His big, strong, battered touch was so gentle. When he trailed his thumb along the edge of my jaw and across my bottom lip, I wanted to curl into his hold and stay there forever.

"I like you. A lot. That's a given, sweetheart," he murmured in that gruff whisper that sent pinwheels of heat dancing over my skin and emotion twisting inside my heart.

His smile was gentle, twisting my heart more sharply. I thought maybe I saw something like what I felt in his eyes, but I wasn't confident to believe in it. When he lifted his other hand and slid it through where my hair fell over my shoulder, one of his fingers spinning in a circle as he idly played with my hair, I could hardly contain myself.

"You know what I mean," I whispered.

The heat in his gaze didn't fade as he dragged his thumb slowly across my bottom lip. "I know what you mean."

"What do we do?" I whispered.

"I don't want to stop," he said.

I knew this was reckless and unwise. Because I was *that* girl—the one who always fell for the wrong guy. In this case, it was beyond foolish because usually, I fell for the assholes. But Haven wasn't an asshole. He was just a good guy whose life had dealt him a few too many gut punches.

"I *really* don't want to stop," he added.

Oh, my little heart, always so hopeful, squealed with joy. I ignored the rest for now because Haven and his whole family were everything I wanted, and I was back home where I felt like I belonged.

When his forehead fell to mine, and he whispered, "We'll figure it out," my chest ached with something tender and terrifying. "Can I kiss you?"

I felt those words on my lips, and my answer was to simply close the millimeters between us and lose myself in another kiss. His mouth was open and lazy, sensual and lingering, and it was a good thing there was a counter behind me, and he was there in front to hold me. Otherwise, I would have collapsed to the floor as I all but swooned.

When we finally broke apart and stared at each other, he trailed his knuckles over my cheek. "You have sand on your face," he said, his lips teasing with a smile.

A giggle slipped out. "I'm sure there's sand everywhere. But I was running late for dinner, and I know your mom likes to have dinner on time." I took him in. "You have some dirt on your cheek."

When a low chuckle rumbled in his throat, I all but swooned all over again inside.

"We could shower," he pointed out. "Together, of course."

The heat in his gaze scorched me just before he stepped back and caught my hand in his.

———

A little while later, I was crying his name as he held me in his arms with my back pressed against the shower wall and my legs curled around his hips. My orgasm broke through me in shimmering waves.

It was only after he dropped his head into the curve of my shoulder that I realized we'd forgotten a condom. A moment later, he lifted his head, smoothing a wet lock of hair off my cheek.

In that second, his eyes widened. "I forgot a condom," he muttered.

"It's okay," I added.

"It is?"

"Yeah, I have an IUD." He was quiet for a long beat. "Going forward, you don't need to worry about it."

His brows hitched up slightly. This was ridiculous. Even now, with him still inside me, I wanted him all over again. With his dark lashes spiky from the water, the blue of his eyes was brighter.

"That's your call," he said slowly.

"And I just called it," I said, feeling a little stubborn about the whole thing.

I felt his chuckle against my chest and bit my lip as I giggled.

"I suppose we could rinse off again," he said when he slowly eased me down, withdrawing as he did.

He reached behind him and turned the shower back on. This had all started after I finished cleaning the sand off my body. We rinsed off in the steamy water and, once again, fell asleep together. That was becoming a habit. While the sexy times made my body sing, it was the intimacy that I felt curled up with him that made me worry about the state of my heart. I kept telling myself that was a problem for another day.

Chapter Twenty-Four

HAVEN

"And this is Chloe," my mom said, gesturing toward the woman in her office.

"Hi, Chloe," I greeted, lifting my hand in a wave.

Chloe smiled up at me. "Nice to meet you, Haven. Looks like I'll be hitting the ground running," she added.

My mom looked pleased as punch. "Elsa already got her all set up, and Chloe is super savvy with computer stuff."

The chime from the front entrance reached us, and my mom glanced between us. "I'll be right back. That's the delivery I'm expecting."

Chloe had a fresh-cheeked prettiness to her, and I took a moment to see if I felt anything. Not because I was even remotely interested, but almost a mental test for myself. Because I hadn't felt anything when it came to women, except for Elsa, since the fire. I couldn't even dredge up the slightest bit of anything other than objective appreciation for Chloe.

Elsa had ruined me.

Even though last night I could have taken the chance to agree with Elsa that maybe things were getting too complicated, I was in *way* too deep. The idea of trying to back out was worse than navigating the treacherous territory we were in.

Chloe had luxurious dark hair in a riot of curls around her face and big, round blue eyes.

"My mom's thrilled to have you here. We all are. We're gonna need you to hit the ground running. But just a heads-up, my mom means well, but she's run this place basically since she was a teenager, back when it was all on paper. Because that's when her parents ran it, and then she helped them. Even when my dad was here with her, they didn't do much online. You'll have to manage her and thread that needle while we modernize."

Chloe's smile was warm. "Got it. I think I can do this."

"Welcome to Heartfire Falls," I said with a chuckle. "Do you need anything from us?"

Just then, Cole appeared in the doorway. "Chloe," he said. "Love the name."

"You do?" Chloe's eyes narrowed.

Cole shrugged. "Yeah. It starts with C, like my name."

Chloe chuckled. "Well, good. I'm glad you like my name."

"And of course, she needs help from us. We don't pull that gender shit around here. You know this, Haven," Cole scolded me as he narrowed his eyes with a mock glare.

Chloe looked between us. "I didn't expect that at all. Your mom said it's kind of an all-hands-on-deck-for-everyone thing."

"Absolutely," I said, narrowing my eyes at Cole. "Anyway, we have a waitlist, or a list, I should say. And all we need is to clear the inspection, which is—"

"Your mom said it was this afternoon," Chloe cut in.

My brows hitched up, but I nodded along. "And I'll be here for that." I glanced toward Cole. "Jude's over at the rescue today."

"Got it. Okay, so we'll both be here for that inspection," Cole replied.

"Great then. Elsa had sort of like a background website set up and waiting for you guys to check out. Do you want to take a look? If you're good with it, I'll just activate it," Chloe said.

"Elsa made a website?" I prompted.

"You don't even realize how amazing Elsa is," Cole said with a brow waggle.

"Oh, but I do," I chimed in.

"Well, you didn't apparently know how amazing," he teased. Cole glanced toward Chloe. "Haven has the hots for Elsa. He's in love with her, but he just hasn't figured it out yet."

I nearly choked and elbowed him hard in the side.

"Where is Elsa, by the way?" he asked.

"She has another job. You know, wildlife biologist," I returned dryly.

"Oh yeah, that's why she's showing up for dinner these days all covered in sand." Cole nodded.

Of course, that comment sent a sizzle of electricity through me, and my mind instantly conjured up the sight of a sandy Elsa stepping into the shower. One thing led to another in my thoughts, and the next thought was Elsa coming all over my cock in the shower.

Fuck my life. I needed to focus.

I cleared my throat. "Let's take a look at that website."

Chloe pressed her lips together to keep from laughing, and she spun her laptop around to click through a few screens.

"Holy shit, this is amazing," Cole exclaimed.

"It is," Chloe agreed. "She did a great job. It's simple but nice. Simple is good because you don't want a complicated website where people get confused. Elsa made the page where people can make reservations and where to find information, and she even linked it to the hotshot firefighter's web page for Willow Brook since you guys help out there." The office phone rang, and Chloe immediately answered. "Heartfire Falls Resort, how may I help you?"

Cole met my gaze and waggled his brows, mouthing, "Professional." I grinned.

"This website really does look amazing," Cole said quietly while Chloe jotted down some information on a notepad.

After she finished the call, she smiled, her eyes twinkling. "You all are popular."

"We were always busy before the fire. It's been a decade, though, so we didn't know how this would go. We gotta get back up and running."

"How do people still know about us?" Cole asked.

"You are too young to recall," I commented. "But we always had a waitlist."

"What do you think of the website?" Chloe asked.

"Publish it. It's perfect," I said.

"Y'all are lucky to have Elsa," Chloe pointed out.

"Haven's *real* lucky to have her," Cole added, his tone sly.

I could see the dare there when I slid my eyes to his. He was all but daring me to protest. I ignored him. "Elsa's amazing. What do you need from us?"

"Well, your mom wants me to start with the reservations and handle all that. She seems to have the supplies under control. I just need to know the scheduling for the hikes and things. How do you handle that?"

"We roll with it," I said. Chloe pressed her lips together, giving me a stern look. "What? We can't just roll with it."

She pulled out a notebook and started flipping through it. "Okay, the Brents want to fish. This other family wants to hike. Another family wants to get flown somewhere. Another group wants fishing, hiking, camping, *and* rock climbing. A group of college students wants..."

"Okay, I get it," I replied, holding up my hand.

"Yeah, we need to be organized. I know they can fish out there in the waterfall, but we need a concrete plan for each trip," Chloe explained.

"We can *all* do all of those things," Cole chimed in.

"Being organized will be a new experience for us," I teased.

"I asked Chloe to organize things," our mom said as she walked into the office, hands on hips. She looked toward Cole first. "Before, we did just roll with it. But it was always a little by-the-seat-of-our-pants kind of thing. I'd like a plan, please and thank you."

"I promised your mama we'd have a plan," Chloe chimed in.

"Where are you from?" Cole asked.

Chloe's sharp gaze shifted to him. "Low country, South."

"Dare I ask what you're doing here?" he added.

"You can dare." Her brows arched up.

"Sheesh, what are you doing in Alaska, Miss Chloe?"

"My daddy loves to fish, so we moved here."

"Well, I think the fishing here is kind of different from fishing in the low country," Cole said slowly.

"Oh, I'm certain it is, and that's why this job is perfect for me. I'm going to learn everything I need to know, so I can take my daddy everywhere." The love in her eyes when she spoke of her father shone as bright as a star in the sky.

"You came to the right place for that," our mom said firmly.

"What's for dinner tonight?" Cole asked.

"He always wants to know what's for dinner," I offered dryly.

"I thought we might order pizza because it's been a hectic day, and I haven't had time to prep anything," our mom said.

"I don't mind driving into town to pick it up," I offered.

"All right, you order enough for everybody." She looked over at Chloe. "Do you want to stay for dinner? You can stay for dinner any night."

"I actually need to get home and make my dad dinner."

"Well, he is also welcome for dinner anytime." My mom shooed us out. "Chloe and I have things to work on. You could watch us, but I'd prefer not."

"Good to meet you, Chloe," I called as Cole and I began to make our way out. "We'll see you around, and we'll come up with a schedule."

Cole nudged me with his shoulder as we walked down the hall. "I gotta go finish up the wiring. It's still funky in the laundry area." Cole was a trained electrician, among other things. "Make sure to get a pepperoni pizza."

"As if I wouldn't get a pepperoni pizza," I deadpanned.

Chapter Twenty-Five

HAVEN

A few minutes later, I was walking out to my truck when my phone vibrated with a text. When I glanced down at it, my pulse started kicking faster when I saw Elsa's name—or rather, Sunny. Because that was what I'd named her in my phone.

Sunny: *Apparently, my battery's dead.*

Me: *I'm headed to town to pick up pizza. You want me to pick you up?*

Sunny: *I'd prefer for my battery not to be dead.*

Me: *We can take care of that later.*

Sunny: *In that case, I'm at my office. It's two streets past Firehouse Café. Take a left on that street, and the office is on the right.*

Me: *I know where the wildlife office is.*

Sunny: *Of course you do, smart-ass. You're Mr. Wilderness.*

Me: *What does that mean?*

Sunny: *Just that.*

I chuckled to myself and resisted the urge to call her for the sole purpose of hearing her voice.

Me: *Should be there in about a half hour.*

I didn't let myself think too hard about the fact that I was smiling almost the whole drive into town.

I called ahead with the pizza order, then stopped to pick up Elsa.

She was waiting outside beside her car. She looked adorable, as always. Her blond hair was up in a ponytail, her cheeks pink. Today, instead of sand, she sported a few streaks of mud on her jeans.

"What'd you do today?" I asked as I approached.

She bit her lip. In a flash, I realized I was already gone for this woman. So fucking gone. All she had to do was smile, and I could have happily stood there in the beam of sun her smile created all day. For *all* of my days.

"I helped with a day camp for third graders. We learned how to dig for clams, hence the mud." She swept her hand up and down her body.

"I see." I stopped in front of her and didn't even resist the urge to kiss her. I dipped my head and laid one on her. She let out a startled exclamation into our kiss but got with the program real quick.

A moment later, I was hard, and we were both breathless when I lifted my head. A low whistle nearby reached us, and Elsa's cheeks got even pinker as she glanced over.

"Hey, Jude," I called.

"Hey, hey, lovebirds," he called in return. "I didn't know you were coming into town."

"I didn't know I was coming into town either," I answered as he stopped beside us.

"I had to go to the hardware store." He thumbed over his shoulder.

The hardware store was on the opposite side of the street. "You crossed all the way over here to spy on us?" I eyed him skeptically.

He chuckled. "No. I just came over because I saw you parking here. Next thing I know, you're kissing." He gestured back and forth between us.

Elsa's cheeks were so red, I could feel the embarrassment emanating from her.

"I like Elsa a lot," I said.

"Okay, so we're not keeping this a secret anymore?" Jude prompted.

"Was it a secret?" Elsa's voice squeaked a little on that last word.

"Not between us. We all suspected," Jude said. "Haven can hardly stop looking at you. Man should be embarrassed."

My brother's gaze softened when Elsa let out a frayed sigh. "Oh, don't you worry. We're all thrilled you're here. Haven's in a much better mood. Please keep rescuing us from his cranky ass."

Elsa giggled, and the sound itself called to my soul and my heart. Elsa made everything better.

"What are you doing at the hardware store?" I asked Jude.

"I'm picking up some lumber for the rescue program."

"You're over there a lot," Elsa observed.

Jude narrowed his eyes at her. "How would you know?"

She rested one hand on a hip, looking sassy. Of course, sassy Elsa sent another shot of blood straight to my cock. I let out a breath and willed my body to cool down.

"Until this week, I was out at the resort all the time. It's none of my business, but you seem a little defensive about it," she pointed out with her brows arched high.

Jude rolled his eyes.

"His best friend works there," I commented.

"Oh, do I know him?" Elsa asked.

"It's Kendall Castille," Jude said. "She moved here in high school, so you probably didn't meet her. And I'm younger than you. You and Haven are the oldies."

"I'm not old," Elsa protested, and Jude chuckled.

"What are you doing in town?" He swung his attention to me.

I didn't miss the fact that Jude was playing it *way* too cool about his bestie. I filed that detail away. "Picking up pizza. Mom's been busy all day with Chloe, who she loves, by the way. That website you made is awesome."

Elsa beamed, and I just wanted to catch her smile and hold it in my heart forever. "Thank you."

"Mom asked me to pick up pizza," I added.

"Good deal. Well, I'll be home in about an hour. Don't eat it all," Jude said.

"First, I need to try to jump-start Elsa's car." We both glanced over. She'd parked with her car practically kissing the building between two other cars.

"Sweetheart, we're going to have to tow that car back to even get to the battery. And I didn't bring my come-along for that," I explained.

Elsa sighed. "I figured. Can I just ride with you, and we'll figure it out tomorrow?"

"Absolutely."

"I'm going to rock and roll. See you two kids at dinner." With a wave, Jude departed.

A few minutes later, Elsa was buckled up in the truck beside me. We kissed two more times, just trying to get in the truck, and it was all I could do not to drag her over the seat and fuck her right here. It was a public place, though, so I started driving to the pizza place.

On the way home, without thinking, I steered down a side road to a private parking spot tucked between some trees.

"What are you doing?" Elsa asked.

"Why don't you come right over here, sweetheart?"

Elsa didn't even hesitate. She started to move before saying, "Just a sec."

Before I knew it, she shimmied out of her jeans. An electric moment later, she straddled me. Her eyes, dark in the barely there light, held mine. I could feel her slippery heat as she rocked over the underside of my length.

"Elsa," I bit out.

"Yes, Haven?" she teased, her voice sly.

I slid a hand into her hair and kissed her fiercely. I broke away, inhaling deeply. "What the hell do you do to me?" I gasped.

The intimacy binding us tighter and tighter felt as if it was spinning around us. The small space in my truck felt filled with the energy created between us.

"I need you." All teasing was gone from her voice. "Inside me."

There was no universe where I could refuse Elsa asking me to fill her, to be joined as closely as I could with her. "Come 'ere."

She rose slightly, and I notched my crown at her entrance, savoring the slick kiss of her heat. I thrust upward as she sank down, sheathing me in the heart of her.

The messy thing was I could try to convince myself this was all about our chemistry, and oh sure, that was part of it. But it was *so* much more.

I'd never expected chemistry to cast a net around my heart, the fiery sparks burning into me, marking me for life, branding me as hers. My heart, my soul, and my body.

As I rocked into her, watching the way her lips parted and feeling the clench of her pussy around me, I knew in my heart her fears about this getting complicated didn't even come close to what it had become for me. When she sank down, her teeth grazed over her bottom lip as she gasped my name, and my heart tattooed her name in a racing beat. The word love was tangled inside of it.

Chapter Twenty-Six

ELSA

Haven's hips rocked up into mine, slow and rhythmic. I was crowded against him, the steering wheel pressing into my back. One knee rubbed against the door and the other against the console. The angle was such that every time he nudged upward, the friction from where we were joined sent pleasure in sharp bursts through me.

This encounter was rushed and raw. Our kisses were open and messy. I could feel the press of his fingers on my hips. I was slippery wet, chasing my release. All the while, even though this felt purely sexual in some ways, sweet hell, I wanted this man so badly and on every level.

When he'd parked a few minutes ago, all I could think was I needed him inside me, fucking me hard and deep. I was *so* gone for him. There was no coming back.

As always, he brought me to the point of begging. "Haven, please..."

"What do you need, sweetheart?" he rasped in that low voice.

"Harder, deeper."

He gave it to me, releasing my hip and sliding his palm up my back to lever me forward just enough that the friction where we were joined felt like a spark catching fire. The pleasure exploded through me.

His name on my lips was the sound of my climax. When he whispered, "That's my Elsa," my heart rioted.

His palm slid down, and I felt the press of his fingers over the flare of my hip as he gasped, "Oh, sweetheart."

We were trembling together as I felt the heat of his release fill me. Afterward, he held me close. The way I felt when he held me—safe and secure as if he alone was holding the world at bay—nearly undid me. I knew I would always be safe with Haven.

I could smell the tang of his day on his skin, a little dusty, a little woodsy, and just him. I traced my fingertip along his collarbone and savored the feel of his fingers sifting through my hair. The intimacy that felt like an actual force between us shimmered in the air when I lifted my head and met his eyes in the falling darkness. He leaned closer to give me a languid kiss.

I could have melted all over. Somehow, we disentangled ourselves. In the cramped space, he helped me put my jeans back on. After that, he drove home through the darkness, one of his hands resting on my thigh as he steered. Fortunately, no one questioned how long it took us to get back with the pizza. Of course, it was fair to say our interlude on the way home fell in the category of quickie.

Yet again, we fell asleep together. In the distant corner of my mind, I worried about how easily he could shatter my heart into a million pieces.

I knew now that I'd never actually had my heart broken before. I just had it bruised, and my pride kicked and scratched a few times. But this man, who was so good and so solid, now held my heart in the palm of his hand. He wouldn't even have to try to break it.

———

The following morning, Haven helped me replace my car battery when he dropped me off at work. I spent the first few hours sifting through data. There were things I loved about being a biologist. I loved the outdoors. I loved the wildlife. I did love the data, although sometimes it made my brain hurt. By the time I took a break, the numbers were blurring.

I finally came up for air after an entire morning deep in spreadsheets, startled to glance at the clock and discover it was early afternoon. My boss stopped in my office. "How're we doing?"

"Good." All I could manage was that vague reply.

"Don't forget to take breaks. Based on how your days have gone so far, you have plenty of flex time."

"Huh?" I drained my now cold coffee.

"Well, you haven't been taking lunch breaks, and you've worked late almost every day so far when you're out in the field."

"I know, but I love it." I smiled, meaning it.

"And I love that you love it, but I don't like you working more than you have to. So just keep that in mind."

"What do you mean, flex time?"

"Well, I can't give you extra leave, but we have flex time. If you don't take lunch or you work late, if it's an emergency and you stay later, you can log it as overtime. Otherwise, you track it and take an afternoon off for appointments or whatever."

"Oh, well, that's good." I paused.

"HR explained that at your onboarding, right?" she eyed me.

"Probably, but I wasn't too focused on all the details." I gave a sheepish shrug, and she chuckled.

"Please don't overdo it. I'm not a stickler about it, but I've seen people burn out too many times over the years. I love an enthusiastic employee, so I don't want you to burn out."

"I need more coffee, so I'll go get some. Do you want some donuts if they still have some? I've fallen deeply in love with the donuts at Firehouse Café."

She grinned. "Always. Just one, though. Don't get a dozen. There are only three of us in the office today."

"You got it."

When I got to the front of the line at Firehouse Café a few minutes later, Luna, the donut-maker in question, smiled at me. "Hey!"

"Hey, I need three donuts and two coffees."

"What kind of donuts?"

"Plain cake, chocolate sprinkles, and rainbow sprinkles."

Luna chuckled. "Coming right up."

Janet came walking out from the back. "Hey, hey," she said with a warm smile.

"Hey, Janet."

"How are things out at Heartfire Falls?"

"Well, I'm working now, so I'm not there all day. They're on track to open soon. They hired an office admin person. It's gonna be wild when they open," I teased.

Janet chuckled. "And, how is Haven?"

I didn't know how Janet knew, but I sensed she knew about me and Haven even though we'd been keeping it very quiet. Of course, my cheeks were burning up. "What do you mean?" I hedged.

She waggled her brows. "Jude might have mentioned something."

"Oh, God," I groaned.

"Oh, wait. Is there gossip?" Luna glanced at us as she turned to slide the coffees across the counter.

"Um, I might like Haven. We might, uh, have a..." I didn't know how to describe what we had.

"A situationship?" Luna offered.

I almost choked on my coffee. "Uh, sure?"

Luna was quiet for a beat, her brown curls bouncing a little when she tipped her head to the side. "You like him."

My heart gave a little spinning kick in my chest. I was well beyond liking Haven. My cheeks still burning up, I nodded.

"Elsa." I glanced over my shoulder.

"Josie?"

Josie grinned. "That's me," she replied in a singsong voice. I glanced at the man standing beside her, who also looked familiar.

"Tate," he offered helpfully.

"Oh, that's right." My brain started to try to gather the details about them.

Josie jumped in, "Yeah, we were like best friends in high school if you recall."

"Wait, are you two together?" I was a little confused.

Josie smiled. "We are. We're engaged."

"To keep it really simple, if you forgot the gossip bonfire, my ex cheated on me with Tate's ex, and Tate's ex was my best friend, and my ex was his best friend."

"Ohhhh," I said slowly.

Josie rolled her eyes. "It's all good. I guess things work out the way they're supposed to."

"How are things going out at Heartfire Falls?" Tate asked.

"They're rolling along. They're planning to open soon."

Tate nodded. "And how's Haven?"

Apparently, Jude was the family gossip. "What do you know?" I blurted out.

He held his hands up. "I come in peace. All I know is Haven totally had a thing for you in high school."

"What?"

While I was busy trying to absorb that knowledge drop from Tate, my phone vibrated, and I glanced down, my lips tugging into a smile solely at the nickname I'd given Haven in my phone.

Big Guy: *I don't know where you are at work, and I hate to ask, but I need someone to pick Tommy up from school and take him to his doctor's appointment. I wouldn't ask except I literally can't leave.*

I was replying before I could even think.

Me: *Of course. Do I just show up at the school and pick him up?*

Big Guy: *Yep. I'll call and make sure you're on the approved pickup list.*

Me: *Are you okay?*

Big Guy: *Equipment issue. There's no way in the universe I'll make it on time. All of us are tied up here, and my mom drove to Anchorage to pick up some stuff from Costco.*

Me: *I'll go right now.*

I glanced around to see several curious gazes on me, just as Luna thrust the donuts at me. "Here you go. They're warm."

"Thank you. I have to hurry. Apparently, I'm picking Tommy up at school and taking him to the doctor."

"That seems like more than a situationship," Luna said with a sly smile.

Chapter Twenty-Seven

ELSA

My cheeks were burning up as I started driving after I made a quick call to my boss to tell her I was taking Tommy to an appointment. I couldn't get over what Tate had said back at the café.

"Haven had a crush on me?" I whispered to myself in the car. "You can't think about this now," I ordered myself as I skidded to a stop in the parking lot at the school.

I didn't know the rules, but I figured I was supposed to go in through the main entrance. I smiled as I walked in because it was the same school I had attended, although it had definitely been upgraded.

When I got to the reception area, Mrs. Wilson glanced up, tipping her head to the side. She looked mostly the same, with just more silver in her hair.

"Mrs. Wilson?" I squeaked.

Her brows hitched up. "That's me. Elsa Whitney?"

"It's me." I felt silly as I smiled at her.

She had always been so sweet to me. I had been, without a doubt, awkward in school. I'd always felt a little out of place. Mostly because, although Alaska was loosey-goosey when it came to the range of people who lived here, the whole off-the-grid lifestyle was fairly far to one side of that range.

"I just want you to know I have all my vaccines." I patted my upper arms with my hands.

She chuckled. "Good to know, sweetheart."

I remembered my parents arguing about that. My dad had wanted my mom to get an exemption, and she had refused.

"I already got a call from Haven Silver, and I understand you're here to pick up Tommy Silver," she added.

I tried to pretend I wasn't blushing. "I'm renting a room out at Heartfire Falls," I offered by way of explanation.

"Honey, you don't need to explain. You're on the pickup list. Tommy's very excited. He thinks the doctor will be more fun with you." She shook her head with a bemused smile.

I snorted a laugh. "We'll see how it goes."

A moment later, she made sure Tommy had his homework in his backpack, and off we went.

"What's this doctor's appointment for?" I asked.

Tommy let out a put-upon sigh. "It's my annual appointment. Dad says I have to go. I already had to go to the lab yesterday and they took my blood. That's more fun than this part."

"It is?" I was genuinely curious.

Tommy's head bobbed enthusiastically. "Yeah, it doesn't hurt and then they have tubes of my blood."

Sliding my gaze to his, I laughed softly. "Well, good for you. Annual appointments are important too."

"Are they, though?" He slid his gaze sideways as I turned onto Main Street.

"Yeah. Take it from someone who knows. They're important."

"What do you mean, 'someone who knows'?"

I pondered what I should tell Tommy. I'd spent enough time with his family to know they took a matter-of-fact approach to the things that happened in life, so I offered the truth.

"I don't know how much you know about my childhood, but I grew up next door to your family. My dad was... well, I loved him a lot, but he didn't believe in modern medicine. He died from pneumonia because he refused to go to the doctor. We'll never know if they could've treated him. As a result, I can never get him back."

Tommy was very quiet before saying softly, "I'm sorry."

"Yeah, I am too. I appreciate that."

"Now I feel like it wasn't nice for me to complain about going to the doctor," Tommy added.

"Oh, that doesn't mean I *like* going to the doctor," I added, casting him a quick smile. "It just means it's important to do these things."

Haven had texted me the directions for where to go, but it was the same family medical office my mother had taken me to, so I knew where it was. Like the school, it had also been updated.

In short order, I was waiting with Tommy in the office after the medical assistant, a friendly woman named Rachel, escorted us in. She tipped her head to the side, her glossy dark hair swinging in its ponytail as she smiled at Tommy.

"This is Elsa," he announced, gesturing to me. "She's here in place of my dad."

Rachel's eyes sparkled as she met my gaze. "Your dad left a message with the receptionist."

"Haven didn't mention that there was anything to be concerned about, and I've never been to a doctor's appointment with a child, so I'm here for moral support," I said quickly.

"That is the most important part," Rachel said. "Do you have any questions or concerns about your health, Tommy?"

Tommy drummed his fingers on his knees. "I keep growing out of my pants, and Grandma says I'm like an empty vessel when it comes to food."

Rachel's lips quirked. "And how much do you eat?"

"As much as I can," Tommy answered honestly.

I bit my lip to keep from laughing.

"All right, kiddo, let's get you on the scale." She glanced toward me. "Tommy's always been healthy. When Haven called earlier, he said everything was status quo."

After she weighed Tommy and checked his height, she announced, "No wonder you're like an empty vessel. There are three more inches of you to feed."

Tommy's eyes went comically wide, and his hair standing straight up in the front gave him an exaggerated look.

There was a light knock on the door, and Rachel called out, "Come in."

A pretty woman with glasses and dark hair with pink-and-purple streaks twisted into a knot came walking in. She looked at Tommy, her gaze quizzical when she glanced toward me.

"This is Elsa Whitney," Rachel explained.

"Tommy's chaperone," I offered.

Tommy thought that was hysterical. "Elsa lives out at Heartfire Falls, and my dad has a crush on her."

Chapter Twenty-Eight

ELSA

My cheeks were probably going to melt off today.

On the heels of a muffled laugh, Rachel cleared her throat. "Elsa, this is Dr. Franklin. She prefers to go by Charlie, or Dr. Charlie."

"Nice to meet you." My voice was squeaky. I was doomed to mortify myself with these women. "I'm Elsa, and I do stay out at Heartfire Falls. I grew up next door, and I just moved back to town. This is my old doctor's office."

"He retired, but I bet your records are still here," Dr. Charlie said, politely ignoring Tommy's teasing about Haven allegedly having a crush on me.

Nobody needed to know that I had *way* more than a crush on Haven.

The doctor reviewed everything with Tommy, checked all his vitals, and proclaimed him the healthiest Tommy Silver she'd ever known in the universe.

At which point, Tommy stood, thrust both fists in the air, and let out a whoop. "I am! Do I get a lollipop?"

Dr. Charlie studied him. "You know, I wanted to get rid of the lollipops because they have a lot of sugar."

"But there have been a lot of complaints," Rachel added, her eyes wide as she emphasized each word dramatically.

"Well, what the f—" Tommy cut in. "The front door?" he corrected at the last minute. "I'm not supposed to swear as much as I do," he added.

Dr. Charlie pressed her lips together. "Learning the appropriate places to say certain words is good."

"You mean swear words?" Tommy pressed.

"Yes. Swear words."

"Do you swear, Dr. Charlie?" he asked next.

Rachel cleared her throat to cover up her laugh.

"I swear sometimes, Tommy. But just like you, I had to learn where I could and couldn't swear. You definitely can't swear in school," Dr. Charlie said, her lips twitching with a smile.

Tommy's sigh was enormous. "I know. That's what my teacher says all the time."

"Do you have any questions, Elsa, before we finish up with Tommy?" She looked over at me.

"I don't think so. I was just making sure Tommy got here because Haven is tied up. I don't really know what happened. Something to do with equipment," I fumbled through my reply.

"Do I get to go out front and pick out my lollipop?" Tommy asked, barely waiting for an answer.

"Go for it," Dr. Charlie waved him out.

He ran so fast I was surprised dust didn't kick up behind him. "It's nice to meet you. I don't think I've met either one of you before. Are you both new to town?" I asked.

"That we are," Rachel replied. "We both came to Willow Brook for different reasons."

"And you know the Silver family?" I asked.

"Hard not to know them. There are six of them. They're all firefighters, at least periodically, and we are both married to firefighters," Rachel said, rolling her eyes. "Word on the street is Haven had a crush on you in high school."

"How does everybody know everything? I didn't know that!" I burst out.

"There's gossip in this town. You're just gonna have to deal with it," Rachel said dryly. "But somebody should lay claim to that man because I might be married, but those Silver boys..." She gave an exaggerated brow waggle. "They're all handsome."

I bit my lip to keep from laughing. "They are."

"So about you and Haven?" she prompted with a lazy circle of her hand in the air.

On the list of things I hadn't been prepared to deal with, it was getting grilled at Tommy's doctor's appointment about Haven. I cleared my throat. "It's possible I have a crush on him too.'"

Rachel bit her lip, grinning with glee. "This is so awesome. Right, Charlie?"

Charlie seemed a little more circumspect than Rachel. She chuckled. "If they want it to be awesome, then yes."

"Anyway, it's really nice to meet you," Rachel added. "I'm sure we'll see you around town."

Just as I opened my mouth to say something, there was a knock on the door. Charlie caught Rachel's eye. "I need to slip out now. I have to get to the next appointment."

As she opened the door, another woman peered through. "Tommy's dad is here."

"Oh!" Rachel exclaimed.

I shrugged while Tommy rolled his eyes, letting out another dramatic sigh as he walked back into the room with his lollipop in hand. He was all about the dramatic sighs today. "He gets very stressed out if he misses my appointments," Tommy said.

"He does?" I asked.

Rachel shrugged. "Bring him on back. We'll give him the update that Tommy's completely healthy, as if that was ever in question."

"You never know," Tommy chimed in.

I bit my lip to keep from laughing.

Rachel gestured toward the woman leaning in the doorway. "This is our new med assistant, Heidi."

"Nice to meet you," I said.

"Like you, Elsa, she just moved back to town."

"You did?" I narrowed my eyes because, surely, I would recognize her.

Her cheeks went a little pink. She was gorgeous, with shiny dark hair twisted into a bun and dangly earrings. "I think I would have been younger than you."

"Do you know me?"

She nodded. "Sorta. You lived out near Heartfire Falls, right?" Before I could reply, she glanced behind her. She gestured into the office. "Tommy and his mom are in here."

Tommy's face split into a mischievous grin. "Should I start calling you Mom?" he asked just as Haven walked into the office. His dark hair looked as if he'd run his hands through it about a hundred times.

Speaking of his hands—those big, strong hands that I loved having all over me—they were dirty and streaked with grease. The med assistant who'd let him in gave him a dimpled smile. "Nice to meet you," she said to me and departed, closing the door behind Haven.

Being the big man he was, he filled this entire space, or that was how it felt. "Sorry I'm late." His eyes flicked to mine. "I caught a ride into town with Jude. Thank you for getting Tommy here."

"No problem."

"I am healthy!" Tommy lifted both fists in the air and bounced his heels against the floor. He'd already finished his lollipop and tossed the stick in the wastebasket by the door.

Haven looked, to say the least, out of place. He dipped his chin in acknowledgment toward Rachel. "Hi there."

"Rachel," she said helpfully. "We've met before. Tommy's doing great. His blood work looks great, he's up to speed on his shots, and we're good to go."

"Okay, so I probably didn't need to rush in."

"Sit, big guy." I patted the chair beside me. Rachel's brows hitched up at that, and my cheeks got hot.

"Is that what you call him?" Tommy asked.

"Sometimes."

Tommy's gaze flicked between us. "I told Rachel you have a crush on Elsa, and that other lady thinks she's my mom."

The tips of Haven's ears turned pink, but that was the only give-away that he was feeling anything at this moment. The man could barely fit in the chair in the doctor's office. He smelled like spruce trees, dust, and fresh air, and I was instantly hot and bothered. *Not the place for it.*

"Do you have any questions for Rachel?" I asked. "Dr. Charlie already saw him and says he's all good. She had another appointment."

Haven shook his head. "Not unless you have any questions for me." He focused on Rachel. "He seems to be growing by the week, maybe even the minute. I can't keep up with the shoes and the clothes. It's a lot."

Rachel bit her lip, and I could tell she was trying not to laugh.

"Go ahead and laugh at the big guy," Tommy offered, spreading his hands wide.

"Kids Tommy's age grow fast," Rachel explained. "And he has tall genes. I've seen all of your brothers around town, and you're all tall."

Haven finally cracked a slight grin and nodded. "We're not short or small."

"Tommy's rate of growth is to be expected. It is what it is. You just have to keep up. Just wait until he hits the teenage years. He won't be growing by the minute. He'll be growing a foot a week," she said with a grin.

Tommy rolled his eyes. "There are fifty-two weeks in a year. I'm not gonna be fifty-two feet tall."

"Thank you for everything," Haven said, standing as Rachel did.

"You are most welcome," she said, her tone soothing. "Now, I need to get to another appointment. So if you don't have any other questions..."

Tommy shook his head, the authority at this moment. "We don't."

Haven chuckled, and I bit my lip to keep from snorting a laugh.

We filed out together. A few minutes later, we were in my car. As I started driving, I realized this was the first time I'd ever had Haven in my car.

"What?" he said when I kept glancing over at him.

"Nothing. I'm just not used to having you in my car."

"Can I ride shotgun? We can switch," Tommy called from the back.

Haven laughed softly as he looked over his shoulder. "No."

He slipped his phone out of his pocket and handed it to Tommy. "You can play your game on the drive home."

"Sweet!" Tommy exclaimed, instantly falling into silence as he focused on Haven's phone.

Haven reached his hand over, placed it on my thigh, and gave me a squeeze. It was all I could do not to wiggle in the seat. Who knew going to a doctor's appointment and having this guy show up would get me all hot and bothered? *But here I was. Absolutely bothered.*

I *knew* Haven could tell. He could read me fairly well.

"Thank you again for getting him to the appointment." Haven's voice was low.

"Anytime."

"I was driving to fix that small walking bridge near the falls and drove over a deep hole, kicked up a rock, and I'm not kidding, it literally punched a hole in my oil pan. Oil everywhere. It's a mess. I can deal with it, but it's a pain in the ass."

I flicked a glance down to his hand. Even though it was filthy, I loved the way it looked on my denim-clad thigh. "I'm sure you'll take care of it. You're handy like that."

His hand slid up, his fingertips trailing along the seam on the inside of my jeans before he rested that big palm right between my thighs. The heat of his touch nearly drew a moan out of me. I bit the insides of my cheeks.

"How was your day?" he asked.

"Busy," I all but choked out.

"Was it okay for you to leave early?" His fingers teased just over where, if he put enough pressure, I might go off like a rocket.

"Don't," I whispered under my breath. When I flicked my gaze to the side and saw his sly grin, I reached down and removed his hand. "It was fine to leave early," I said in response to his question. "My boss told me I have flex time, which apparently they told me at my onboarding, but I didn't pay enough attention."

"You do get distracted sometimes." At that sly comment, his hand slid back up between my thighs.

I sucked in a breath, trying to cool the heat suffusing me. Pointless, but I could try.

He cleared his throat, letting out a sigh. "What did you do today?"

I didn't even know what he was talking about. "Huh?"

"What did you do today?" he repeated. "You know, at work, wildlife biology and all that."

Chapter Twenty-Nine

HAVEN

"You're gonna pay for this," Elsa whispered under her breath before launching into a dry explanation about some kind of spreadsheet and analyzing data.

Tommy was blissfully occupied in the back, although his presence was the only reason I didn't try to make a move on Elsa.

When we got back home, he handed me my phone as he climbed out of the car, dashing toward the rescue program. Elsa put her car in park and whipped her gaze toward mine, her cheeks flushed pink and her eyes dark.

"You asshole," she hissed.

"I need to show you something." I removed my hand from between her thighs and caught hers, placing it over my thick length.

"Haven..." She sounded breathless, and I enjoyed that too much.

She let out a laugh, her head falling back against the seat as she gave me a squeeze. My cock pulsed under her touch.

"Haven Silver, you're going to kill me," she said flatly.

"Well, we definitely don't want that," I said, my voice a dry rasp.

Rolling her head to the side, she locked her eyes with mine. The desire flashing there tightened every cell in my body. "Let's go," she said.

Moments later, we scrambled out of her car, stumbling up the stairs. Once we made it inside, I bent her over the kitchen counter.

I knew, I really, *really* did, that I was in over my head. I was *so* fucking gone for Elsa. She had no clue I'd been half in love with her in high school. She had no clue how much I'd missed her after she was gone, even though it was just stolen glances in those days.

There were so many things she didn't know, and she'd think I was crazy. All these years, I convinced myself it was just a little crush. Except her sweetness had always shined through, and then I turned into a grumpy jerk, hurting from the pain of compounding losses.

Now, here she was, thinking this was just some kind of convenient arrangement because we had such good chemistry. Although there was no adjective sufficient for how hot and fast our chemistry burned. It wasn't burning away; it was only burning hotter. The more I had her, the more I wanted her.

Yet Elsa didn't know, and I had to somehow keep my shit together. Somehow persuade her this could be more. I didn't even know how to do that.

Chapter Thirty

ELSA

I was startled to glance down at the text from my mother.

Mom: *I'd love to visit.*

"What?"

"Everything okay?" Maggie asked from where she was rinsing plates in the sink and putting them in the dishwasher.

"I texted my mom to invite her to visit, and she said she'd come. I'm just a little surprised," I replied.

Maggie turned, reaching for the dish towel and drying her hands before crossing over and giving me a quick hug. There was no shortage of hugs when it came to Maggie Silver. She squeezed my shoulders as she stepped back. "I'm so glad."

I took a quick breath. "She hasn't been here since we left."

Maggie knew this, but I was almost talking myself through it.

"I know. Your dad and your mom loved each other very much. I'm sure the idea of coming back here was painful after he passed."

"Well, that and—" I shook my head slightly. "He didn't have to die."

Maggie pressed her lips together as she rested her hips against the counter. "People are complicated. And who knows what he thought at the end? I will never stop being so sorry that you happened to be alone with him when he actually did pass." She let out a sigh. "He was just..."

"Stubborn," I finished for her.

"I don't know how else to put it. And misguided. Alaska is the promised land for people like your father. They want to live off the grid and do it all on their own. Except they don't realize how much even the idea of thinking you can do it all on your own is a privilege in our world today."

"I know. So many things that support us are invisible." A sigh slipped out. "My dad didn't think modern medicine could help anyone."

"Pneumonia can kill people, as he learned. I'm glad your mom is coming to visit. She probably won't stay long-term, but a visit is good," Maggie said.

I knew my mom wouldn't ever return to live here, but I was glad she'd finally visit.

"When you talk to her, tell her I said hi. And of course, she is always welcome here," Maggie said.

I didn't realize I was crying until Maggie reached for a box of tissues and thrust it toward me. I swiped at my tears with my fingertips and blew my nose.

"Thank you. You all welcoming me here and letting me stay has made coming back so much less complicated."

"Sweetheart, we're happy you're here." A sly glint entered her eyes. "And I'm very happy about you and Haven."

"Really?"

"You know that boy had a crush on you when you two were in high school."

"What?" I sputtered.

She rolled her eyes. "Tell him I told you to ask him about it."

I'd had a long day at work, hiking along a trail with one of the interns to clear old markers and install new ones. Haven had just come in, exhausted after working all day.

After he came out of the shower, my body hummed. Good grief, he was unfairly sexy. He wore a pair of loose sweatpants and no shirt.

I was instantly distracted, or rather, my hormones were. But I had a mission, and curiosity was getting to me. "Your mom told me to ask you something," I said.

He filled a glass with water and took a swallow. "What's that?"

I bit back a sigh. Even the flex of his forearm as he lowered the glass was sexy. "She said you had a crush on me in high school."

He tipped his head to the side, pressing his tongue in his cheek before sliding it across his teeth. "I did." He looked a little sheepish.

"Really?" I squeaked, resting my elbows on the counter.

"Oh, most definitely, Elsa. You were *that* girl. You *are* that girl."

My mouth dropped open. "I can't believe it."

"Believe it," he pressed.

He set the glass down and took two steps toward me. Breathless, I turned to face him. Whenever he was close like this, I felt encompassed, protected, and turned on. I loved it. My palm landed on his chest, only to discover his heart was beating as hard and fast as mine.

"You were the girl next door."

"Next door in Alaska isn't all that close," I pointed out.

His chuckle sent goose bumps chasing over my skin. "Maybe. But then you showed up at the high school, and there you were, like a ray of sunshine."

He lifted a hand, trailing the back of his knuckles over my cheek and down the side of my neck. I almost purred aloud, nearly shivering at his touch.

"With these freckles..." His thumb traced over my bottom lip. "And these lips. You were so cute."

"Oh." That was all I could manage before he dipped his head and kissed me.

Chapter Thirty-One

HAVEN

Walking into the kitchen, I snagged the moment in front of me. My mom was rarely alone in the kitchen and always on the move.

"So..."

She glanced over. "What is it?"

I got straight to the point. "You told Elsa I had a crush on her in high school."

My mom was entirely unabashed and shrugged casually. "I sure did. I mean, you *did* have a crush on her in high school."

"I did," I admitted slowly.

Her gaze sobered as she studied me. "I'm really glad Elsa came back. Even more than that, I'm glad you two are together."

I took a slow breath. "I think I love her."

"Oh, you love her," my mom said flatly. "You absolutely love her."

"I don't want to mess it up."

"You won't. Oh, it won't be perfect. There is no perfect. Ever. It's about finding someone who you can ride those choppy waters with and stay afloat together."

"I miss Dad."

My mom's eyes shone with a glint of tears. "I do too. And I miss Bree so much."

"Sometimes it hurts." I swallowed through the rush of emotion balled in my throat.

"It means the world that you fought for us to be able to get this place back and rebuild it. Your brothers have helped so much. But I know we made it this far because you fought with the insurance company, and you won those battles."

I let out a breath slowly. "I love you, Mom."

She squeezed me tight when she hugged me, then stepped back, patting me on the cheek. "And I love you. Now go be good to that girl you love. It was just a crush back in the day, but now it's real."

"I know," I said, that knowledge both freeing and terrifying.

———

A few days later

I was just paying for my coffee when I caught the scent of smoke. I glanced around, not seeing anything.

"Do you smell that?" I asked Casey as she handed me my change.

"Oh, I'm sure it's something in the kitchen." She peered into the kitchen, turning to glance over the waist-high door. "Huh, don't see anything."

As my gaze arced about the space, I noticed smoke seeping through one of the vents to the upstairs.

"Where are the stairs?" I practically barked out. "And we need to —" The smoke alarms began blaring. "Get everybody out. Now. Who's upstairs?"

"Janet, I think. I don't know!" Casey spun in a circle.

"You get everybody out. Where are the stairs?"

Casey pointed me toward the back, and I bolted, rushing around the counter into the kitchen.

"Stairs!" I called to Luna, who looked at me with wide eyes. "Help Casey make sure everybody gets out of here. I think there's a fire upstairs."

The smoke was thick in the stairwell as I dashed up.

"Janet!" I called when I heard her coughing as I crested the top of the stairs.

"I'm fine!" she yelled out.

I strode quickly down the short hallway up there. The smoke was thick and hot. I scooped Janet into my arms. "Wait!" she demanded.

"We can wait after I get you out of here." I shouldered my way down the narrow hallway and down the stairs.

Once I set her on her feet outside, she looked up at me, her eyes wide with worry. "My cat! I—"

"Where's your cat?" I asked as I passed her over to the EMTs, who must've zoomed down here from the station. Considering they were housed less than half a mile away, it was possible.

"In my office in the back," Janet said between coughs.

I turned right back around and went in. No one else was left inside, which meant Luna and Casey had hustled everyone out. Thank God.

Blessedly, wherever the hell this cat was, it had things to say and was meowing wildly, its annoyance clear. I found the cat pressed up against a window in a tiny office at the back of the upstairs. I scooped the cat into my arms. I could barely breathe. The smoke was thick and the heat intense as I raced down the hallway again.

When I got outside and Janet saw her cat, her eyes welled with tears.

"He's not thrilled with the situation," I said.

Janet wiped at her tears while Dana, the EMT, continued checking her over.

"He seems fine," I offered. I glanced toward Firehouse Café while Janet focused on her cat.

"She's good to go," Dana offered.

I glanced at Dana. "Pretty sure Janet is indestructible."

Janet glanced between us. "Of course I am."

"They're going to put the fire out, but there will be some damage," I commented, glancing over at the town's fire truck. The local crew was fast at work, containing the fire.

"All these years, and I've been so lucky." Janet sighed as she stroked her cat.

"What do you mean?"

"No kitchen fires, nothing. And now this."

"Do you know what started it?" I asked.

She shook her head. Dana had rounded the ambulance to check on something in the front, and I rested a hand on the back door as I studied Janet. "You're feeling okay?"

"I'm fine. Thank you for carrying me out, though I think that was unnecessary." Her tone was pointed.

"And Chunky," she offered. She gestured toward her cat, happily purring in her arms now.

"Chunky is safe." I chuckled. "That's all that matters. Do you need a ride anywhere?"

She narrowed her eyes. "Haven, I can drive. I'm a little smoky, but I'm fine."

I lightly squeezed her shoulder. "Good."

I jogged over to the town's fire truck. Susanna, who headed up the crew for the town, met my gaze.

"We've got it under control." She looked emotional, but we all were. Firehouse Café was the nerve center of town, a place of nothing but goodness. It was also the old fire station from years back.

"Damage doesn't look too bad," I offered.

"No, but—" Susanna let out a breath. "Something feels off about this."

"What do you mean?"

"No fire in the kitchen, which is what we'd expect. It started upstairs."

"Electrical, maybe?"

She shrugged. "Best guess. Anyway, thanks for running upstairs to get Janet and her cat."

I shrugged. "I was here. Literally."

———

Within the hour, the fire was declared out. Many residents from town had gathered in the parking area at Firehouse Café.

"Haven!" At the sound of Elsa's voice, I glanced around.

"What happened?" She stopped beside me.

I wasn't even thinking when I curled an arm around her shoulders and leaned down to press a kiss on her forehead. Her cheeks were pink when I lifted my head.

"What?" I asked.

She shrugged, wrinkling her nose. "It's not a secret anymore because of Jude, but I think that's our first PDA."

"About time," Janet chimed in. She stopped beside us, her smile warm.

"About time for what?" I asked lightly.

"You two. Just be open about it. I'm happy for you both."

"Are you okay, Janet?" Elsa's gaze was concerned.

"I'm fine. There's some damage upstairs, but we'll get it fixed. The downstairs is completely fine. I've already checked with the town. We have to do a few things to pass the safety inspection, but I should be able to reopen in another day or so." Janet's tone was determined.

"Where's Chunky?" I asked.

Janet chuckled. "I drove him home. He's not thrilled."

"Who's Chunky, and are you sure you're okay?" Elsa asked.

Janet reached over and squeezed Elsa's shoulder. "My cat, who hangs out upstairs when I'm working. Stop worrying about me."

"Janet! You're everyone's favorite. We're going to worry about you," Elsa protested.

Janet grinned. "I'm fine. And your big guy here"—she gestured to me with a brow waggle—"rescued us both."

"Is that why you smell like smoke?" Elsa asked.

"That would be it," I said dryly.

Janet moved along, chatting with various people clustered outside of the café.

"Wow. I wonder what happened," Elsa mused.

"I'm sure they'll do an investigation. Janet seems okay, and no one got hurt. That's all that matters," I said.

Elsa shook her head slightly as we looked over at Janet. "Janet is the living, breathing definition of resilient. Did you really carry her out?"

"I was getting coffee when we smelled smoke, and the smoke alarms went off. I told Casey and Luna to get everybody out. I went upstairs, and that's where Janet was. She was out of breath from the smoke, so I carried her down. Then I went back up to get her cat." I took a breath, letting it out. "I'm just glad they're both okay."

"I'm glad you're okay too," Elsa added.

"Of course I'm okay."

"It's never 'of course,'" Elsa pointed out.

I knew what she meant. Dipping my head, I brushed my cheek against hers as I breathed in her scent. "Should we go home?" I asked when I lifted my head.

Chapter Thirty-Two

ELSA

Should we go home?

Of course, I nodded when Haven asked that. Alaska was home. Willow Brook was home. And now, Heartfire Falls Resort in this small apartment above a barn was home.

Haven felt like home. I was falling. So hard and fast. For a person and a place. I was in *way* too deep.

I'd always felt a little bit out of step with everyone. For most of my life, I'd wanted nothing more than to feel like I belonged somewhere. Haven and Heartfire Falls gave me that feeling.

I fell asleep in Haven's arms that night after he took me roughly in our bed. Being with him felt so good it almost frightened me. The goodness felt as fragile as spun sugar.

The next evening, Chloe walked into the kitchen where we were eating and announced, "Some guy is here looking for Elsa."

I should have known it would all blow apart. The goodness cracked on the edges. I'd always known it had to be too good to be true.

"Huh? Who?" I asked.

"He says his name is Brad," Chloe replied.

A ball of ice and dread formed in my stomach instantly. I was relieved Haven was running late and blessedly not present for this.

"I don't like the name Brad," Tommy announced. He took his last bite of cereal, and the sound of his spoon dropping against the edge of the bowl clattered on my unsettled nerves.

"What should I tell him?" Chloe asked, oblivious to my state.

I swallowed. "I'll deal with it."

Jude happened to be standing by the doorway, and his eyes met mine. "You okay?" he asked as I walked by.

"Fine," I said, knowing my tone was sharp. I took a shaky breath as I walked through the resort to the main entrance, all the while wondering how the hell Brad had found me.

I wasn't sure as I approached if Chloe had left him waiting on the porch. I kind of hoped she had. When I discovered the door was closed and no one was waiting in the entryway, I let out a tiny sigh of relief.

I was over Brad.

You are over Brad.

Great, now we're talking to ourselves in the third person. Even worse, we're referring to ourselves like we're a split personality or something.

I mentally chastised myself. I *was* over Brad, but I was still disappointed in myself. Deeply embarrassed because he'd played me for a fool, and it hadn't even taken much effort on his part. I knew this. My track record with men was so pathetic.

After we moved away from Willow Brook during high school, I'd been that foolish young girl who wanted to fall in love and was so desperate to belong. Even though my parents' marriage had actually been a decent example—my dad had adored my mom—the world wasn't all that kind to girls like me.

I'd been insecure and felt out of place everywhere I went. All of that had led to a string of stupid choices when it came to men. These choices culminated in Brad, the big boss of assholes in my life.

My hands were damp from nervousness and anxiety. I brushed them over the front of my jeans, cleared my throat, and swung the door open. I didn't even give Brad a chance to think he could come in.

I stepped onto the porch, closing the door behind me. "Hi, Brad." My voice was a little loud, a little forced.

He tipped his head to the side, his lips curling in a slow smile. That smile once would have gotten to me. Now, it just made me feel angry.

"Elsa, Elsa, Elsa," he said, using what I thought of as his fake charming voice.

I crossed my arms. "What is it, Brad?"

"Babe, I missed you." His voice was low, cajoling.

I took a minute to study him. The man was handsome. He had brown hair shot through with gold—not quite blond, but almost. He also had blue eyes, and he was really good at making them look wide and innocent, like he did now.

Haven's blue eyes were better. I silently scoffed. "Brad, what do you want?"

I didn't even give in to the urge to pointedly tell him that I didn't miss him. Because I didn't. It was so *not* fun to be involved with someone who constantly elicited a sense of insecurity. Brad had been that guy—handsome, intelligent, had a good job. He had it together on the surface yet had played me like the foolish fiddle I was.

For better or worse, my abandonment issues—say, my dad dying and leaving us nearly broke—made me crave stability in an unhealthy way. Grief was messy most of the time.

Brad's gaze sobered, and he stuffed his hands in his pockets, shifting from the guy who was worried about me and missed me to looking a little contrite. "I mean it, Elsa. I missed you."

I tightened my arms in front of my chest. "You didn't miss me, Brad. What do you want? I don't have anything you want, so I have no idea why you're here and why you even chased me down."

Shocker of all shockers, he decided to play it straight. "I'll be honest. I heard you inherited that property here and—"

"What do you need with that property?" I cut in.

"Collateral."

"Collateral?" I sputtered. All that hurt and foolishness spun like an angry, painful storm in my chest.

"Fuck off, Brad. Just leave." I turned to go just as Brad reached for my arm, his hand closing around the spot above my elbow a little too tightly. I sensed motion just out of the corner of my eye.

I glanced over to see Haven practically running as he dashed up onto the steps. "Get your fucking hands off her," he nearly growled.

Brad had already dropped his hand because I'd yanked my elbow away.

"Who the fuck are you?" Brad muttered. He was used to being in control and calling the shots.

"I own this place, and I'm telling you right now to get the hell off this property." Haven met my gaze. "Who is this?"

"Brad, my ex. He's an asshole. He wants my property. For collateral," I said, my tone dry.

"Jesus, Elsa. I'm not that bad," Brad protested.

I felt on the verge of tears. Not because I was sad about Brad. But his presence and being so blunt about the property—that was how little he thought of me. I hated how stupid I felt.

"Get the hell out of here," Haven spoke to Brad dismissively.

When I glanced between the men, the contrast couldn't have been more stark. While Brad was handsome, it was polished and calculated. Haven was everything he wasn't. Brad used an attitude and superficial confidence to make it seem as if he was assured. Haven was the real deal. He was in shape, not because he worked out, but because his life demanded it. His strength was rugged and assured because his life demanded that too. He fought fires. He led hikes through the wilderness. He was all rugged and pure man. None of it an affectation. All of it deeply real.

Even in this brief interaction, it was clear that Brad knew there was no sense in trying to make it seem like anything else. It was like watching two male dogs circle each other, and Brad ran off with his tail between his legs. He held his hands up, taking a step back. "Whoa, buddy. Back off."

Haven eyed him steadily. I could practically hear a silent growl in his throat. "I don't know what the fuck you want, but—"

Then Brad tried to go and be stupid. "Don't overdo it, tough guy."

Haven didn't even move. "I'm a lawyer. I'll bury you in lawsuits if you don't get off my property right now."

I often forgot that detail about Haven. He didn't talk about it much.

Brad was quiet for a few beats. Haven moved, taking one step in his direction. Brad blanched. "Calm the fuck down, man. I'm out of here."

I didn't realize my eyes were welling up with tears until Brad was climbing into his car, and Haven turned to face me.

"Sweetheart, what's going on?"

I blinked. I felt like even more of an idiot because I should have handled this myself. I didn't need some guy swooping in to straighten it all out for me. Yet it only made me love Haven more. He had no idea what a mess I was.

I opened my mouth to say something, anything, and I couldn't. All I could do was turn, shake my head, and tighten my arms around my waist. "I have to go."

"Elsa, wait!" Haven called as I turned.

Chapter Thirty-Three

HAVEN

I jogged down the steps, catching up to Elsa in a few strides. She spun back.

"I just need some time to myself. It's fine, I promise. I'm fine," she insisted.

It was all I could do not to reach for her arm, but I just chased off a guy who grabbed her arm, so I wasn't about to do that. I watched quietly as she turned and hurried away. One of the goats had gotten loose and trotted over to her, headbutting her in the knee. She leaned down to pet Dolly before walking off.

I stood there, looking toward that vehicle that just left, shiny and black. Maybe a little dusty from the drive down our road, but that was it.

Cole's voice reached me. "What's up?" he asked as he approached.

I pondered Brad, Elsa's ex. I didn't know what the hell to think about that. We hadn't defined anything, but I knew my feelings. I sensed Elsa had no idea how much she meant to me.

Over the following days, it became clear that whatever happened with that guy built a wall between Elsa and me. Oh, she didn't stay out of our nights. We were still tangled up in the sheets every night, but I could feel the distance. When we were skin to skin, her heart was barricaded away.

As usual, I was so busy I barely had time to breathe, much less ask her what the hell was going on.

"What's wrong with you?" Tommy asked one morning.

"What do you mean?"

He rolled his eyes dramatically. "Well, ever since that day that guy came, you've been weird. You're not as nice as you were with Elsa. What happened?"

He wasn't wrong on that count.

I tried to talk to Elsa a few times, but she didn't let any conversation go past the surface. A few days passed, and I stopped in at Firehouse Café with Jude to check on Janet and see how things were going after the fire upstairs. A hint of smoke lingered in the lower part of the café.

Luna glanced up as she handed me a donut. "For you."

"I didn't order one."

"I know, but you helped Janet and her cat. So free donuts forever."

I chuckled. "Luna, I can't take free donuts forever."

"Why the hell not?" Jude asked from my side.

I slid my gaze to my brother. "Because if I have free donuts forever, you guys are going to be on me all the time to bring them to you by the dozen."

Luna's lips curled in a bemused smile. "Fair point. Okay, one single free donut for you *only*, whenever you come in."

Jude narrowed his eyes at her. "Are you serious?"

She rested a hand on her hip. "Absolutely. Did you carry Janet and Chunky out?"

Jude rolled his eyes with a bemused smile. "I wasn't here, so I don't think it can be held against me that I didn't."

Luna gave a saucy shrug. "Just tell me your favorite, Haven, and I'll make sure to set one aside for you."

"How is Janet?" I asked.

"I'm fine," Janet replied in a singsong voice as she came out from the back and rounded the counter to pull me into a lung-squeezing hug. When she stepped back, her eyes crinkled at the corners with her smile. "Haven Silver, my hero."

I thought Jude might choke. "God help us. Please don't call him a hero."

"He *is* my hero, though," Janet said with a wide grin. "He's your hero too, you know."

Jude let out a sigh. "I know."

Jude didn't talk about it much. Hell, we all hated talking about the fire, but I had actually dragged him out during the wildfire at the resort. We chatted briefly before I asked, "Any updates on what caused the fire upstairs here?"

"Electrical," Janet said simply. "This building is old and while I've updated just about everything downstairs, I haven't updated anything up there. An old fuse blew and set it off." She paused and shrugged. "No one got hurt, so it's my reminder to get things taken care of." Janet's ability to roll with the punches of life was legendary and she didn't even dwell.

She shifted topics and tossed some unwelcome gossip at my feet. "So some guy's nosing around about Elsa's property."

"Some guy named Brad?" I countered quickly because I knew exactly who it had to be. "How did you hear about that?"

"I hear about everything, Haven," Janet said matter-of-factly. "And of course, I'm old friends with one of the attorneys at Blackthorne Law. He doesn't handle my cases, but he let me know that it came out of nowhere. Who is this Brad guy?"

"Haven refers to him as *the asshole*," Jude offered.

"I'll agree on that count because unless Elsa wants to sell—" Janet began.

"Elsa doesn't want to sell," I ground out. "To make it really brief, he's her ex, and for some reason, he wants that property for collateral. I have no idea why."

"It's not the property here. She owns a piece of property in Anchorage." Janet narrowed her eyes. "My lawyer friend told him Elsa isn't interested."

"Dude, don't crack a tooth," Jude said from my side.

I had to consciously unclench my jaw. I didn't know exactly what this guy had done to Elsa, but I knew he had hurt her. I was sure she was well over him, but I didn't like him showing up like this.

My train of thought was interrupted by Jude. "Haven might be jealous."

"I'm not fucking jealous," I muttered.

"Testy?" Jude clucked at my side.

"What? Just, ugh." I let out a groan, pinching the bridge of my nose briefly. "I'll handle it."

"Handle what? There's nothing to handle," Jude pointed out.

I narrowed my eyes at him. "Do me a favor, Janet. If you can scrounge up that guy's number, I'd appreciate it."

Jude walked out with me a few minutes later, stopping at the back of my truck. "I'd like to point out that I don't think Elsa would like you handling her business like this."

"There is no business to handle. I'm just making sure he leaves her the fuck alone," I said.

Although his comment gave me a twinge of hesitation, I was too pissed off about Brad to listen to that twinge.

Hours later, in the resort kitchen

"What?" she yelped, spinning around. "Haven, why would you do that?" She held her phone in her hand, her eyes scanning the screen.

"Oh, for fuck's sake," Jude muttered from my side.

"I'm not talking to him, but Brad left a message that *you* called him." Elsa pinned her gaze on me.

"Elsa, you made it clear you weren't interested in selling whatever it is that you own in Anchorage."

"I just own a rental property. I got it from my mom. It was my dad's. I guess it was in a trust with her for years, and now it's mine. I don't do anything. There's a property management company that handles it." She blinked and shook her head.

"You made it clear to Brad—" Defensiveness rose like a blind wall inside me. "Look, I don't like that guy."

"Yeah, well, I don't either. But what the hell are you doing, Haven?

I can handle my own stuff." She let out something between a growl and a groan and narrowed her eyes at me before flinging the dish towel on the counter. "I need some space."

"Elsa." I started to chase her, but fucking Jude and Cole were right there.

"Wouldn't do that, man. Told you," Jude said from behind.

Chapter Thirty-Four

ELSA

Maggie and Chloe listened to my little outburst as I finished with, "And I was going to deal with it."

Maggie let out a soft sigh before pulling me into a quick hug and squeezing my shoulders as she stepped back. "Haven likes to take care of people, and he doesn't always know when to back off." She let out another sigh. "But my gut tells me there's a little bit more to this than that."

"What do you mean?" I chewed the insides of my cheeks to the point of pain. Just thinking about the *more to this* brought up all of my embarrassment and foolishness inside.

"I'm not asking you to explain your reaction, but I'm curious." Maggie eyed me carefully. "All Haven did was what you say you want, which is for him to back off."

"What's the other guy's name again?" Chloe asked.

"Brad," I ground out.

"That's a good asshole name," Chloe replied, and I burst out laughing.

"Haven loves you," Maggie said, her gaze somber.

My heart was beating so hard, the echo of it reverberated to every cell in my body, and I wanted to cry. "Okay."

Maggie's phone rang, and she had to take the call. Everything was hectic and crazy here because they were opening in a week. She hurried away, mouthing, "Don't forget he loves you."

I didn't even realize my tears had started to flow until Chloe stuffed some tissues into my hands. "For what it's worth, Maggie's right. It's plain as day. Haven loves you. You know what you need?"

"What?" I sniffled.

"A girls' night."

Aside from my massive, overwhelming fears about abandonment and putting myself out there, what if I made a fool of myself with Haven? Maybe he did love me. But he sure as hell didn't have time for more than what we already had, which was some really smoking-hot benefits at night. Here I was worrying about how much time he had, as if *that* was the problem.

"Elsa?" Chloe prompted.

"Huh?"

Chloe blinked as her gaze coasted over my face. "I was invited out to, I guess, a regular get-together they have. Just women, and you need support. There's nothing like the support of a whole group. It's a collective energy thing." Chloe was completely serious.

A twinge of guilt pricked my conscience. "Oh, that's right. Tiffany invited me before, but I couldn't go because—" Pausing abruptly, I let out a sigh. "No good excuse. I always worry I don't belong, so I didn't go and gave her some lame reason."

Chloe narrowed her eyes, resting a hand on her hip. "Stop it," she said.

"Stop what?"

"Look, Elsa, I might be new here, but here's the thing about Alaska: everybody's a little funky here. I bet it was hard to move in the middle of high school like you did because what few connections you had were taken away. You probably felt really out of place wherever you went to high school after that. Where was that?"

"Seattle," I said.

"Whoa, talk about a change of pace. Major urban center. Anyway, my new friend Josie invited me, and she told me I could bring someone if I wanted. You're my plus-one." She smiled, but her eyes had a bossy look. "So you're coming, and we are all going to give you moral support."

I blew my nose, took a shaky breath, and nodded. Even though it felt dramatic, I put a note on my bedroom door that Haven was not allowed to come in because I needed a little time to think things over. I figured putting it there now was a little insurance that I'd take the space I needed.

———

"I remember you." Josie pulled me into a big hug.

Josie was an Olympic skier, so it was kind of hard not to know who she was in our little world. All that aside, her smile was warm, she was welcoming and kind, and before I knew it, I'd gotten about ten hugs from everyone there.

Aside from Chloe and me, Josie, Maisie, Amelia, Madison, Tish, Luna, and Casey were here.

"We're a smallish group tonight," Tish pointed out.

Before I could even reply to that, four more women piled in. Respectively, Phoebe, Lucy, Stella, and Rachel.

"See? You're not the only new person here," Chloe said with a pointed look, promptly followed by a squeeze around my shoulders.

"Do not *ever* worry about that," Madison said, who was, honestly, intimidatingly beautiful with her glossy dark hair, sparkly green eyes, and almost regal features.

"Yeah, we all look at her like that," Amelia offered dryly from my side.

"Huh?" I glanced askance.

"She used to be a homecoming queen," Maisie added.

"Hey." Madison held up a hand. "I'll have you know that maybe I *was* a homecoming queen in high school, but I've come a long way since then. I can now chop wood, start a fire, survive potential hypothermia..." She let out a sigh, rolling her eyes slightly. "Graham even asked me to help him when he butchered a moose."

I couldn't keep the snort of laughter from escaping. "And, how did that go?"

"Oh, it went," she said dryly. "I've never done anything like it."

"You know, that *is* something I've done," I chimed in. "My dad was big on moose hunting and fishing and more."

"You grew up here?" Madison prompted, her voice lilting in question.

"I did."

"Remind me, when did you move away?" Phoebe asked.

"Well, after my dad passed in my sophomore year in high school."

"Oh, that's right." Phoebe's brow wrinkled with worry. "I'm sorry about your dad," she added.

"I appreciate that. It's been years, so I've had time to get used to it."

"Are you planning to rebuild on your parents' old property?" Amelia asked.

I shrugged, throwing my hands up and letting them fall. "That's the plan. But it's kind of a long-shot plan. For now, I'm staying at Heartfire Falls."

"And Haven's in love with her," Chloe interjected, *sooooo* not-helpfully.

"Chloe!" I yelped.

She shrugged, clearly not feeling any guilt about putting my business in front of this whole group.

Josie's smile was warm from across the table. "He totally is. Let's just be honest."

"I sense a story. What is it?" Madison asked.

I tried not to cry, although I could feel the tears threatening and had to blink them away. "He's being a little overbearing." I quickly summarized the whole situation about Brad, ending with, "And Haven butted in. I can deal with it."

"What's the deal with Brad?" Maisie asked.

"He's my ex, and he's an asshole. It's kind of my specialty, dating assholes." I let out another sigh. "It's been a long time, but I'm sure you all remember, my dad was..." I tapped my fingers on the table.

"Quirky? His quirkiness is what killed him. I'm all about people being a little offbeat, but he died because of his own stupidity. Drives me nuts. Anyway, even though he grudgingly let my mom send me to school, I never really got to have regular friendships or date. It wasn't because he was controlling. He was just a dumbass." I rolled my eyes. "To be honest, I was always embarrassed about bringing people out for a slumber party or something like that, and he was always worried about me being exposed to, you know, regular life. God love the man. He was a sweetheart but totally misguided. All this to say, I don't think it helped me with my judgment in men, mostly because I just wanted the chance to have regular things in my life. So it's not like Brad was anything unusual, except that he just took advantage of me. I have no idea how he found out about me owning the property in Anchorage. Now, he wants to use it as collateral." I shrugged. "But it's the kind of thing he would want to do."

"I don't like Brad." Josie narrowed her eyes.

"I don't either. Not even a little," Amelia said.

"So let me get this straight. You're upset with Haven for getting in the middle?" Phoebe prompted.

"I guess. I can deal with Brad. I really can," I insisted.

"Of course, you can," Madison said matter-of-factly. "But what's wrong with Haven helping? Based on what you've described, Brad seems like the kind of guy who would back off more easily with a man. Sometimes it's helpful. Haven can use his privilege in a good way."

I nodded slowly. "Okay, that makes sense."

"Like, say in a bar fight, I'm not that tall," Lucy pointed out. "It's probably helpful if somebody bigger than me gets in the middle of it. Brad isn't physically threatening you, but he sounds like a class-A asshole who might pull some shit behind the scenes. And Haven's an attorney, even though we all kind of forget that. He's also a tough guy."

"I wouldn't mess with him," Maisie offered with a wry smile.

"I know, right?" I let out a little snort. "I do forget he's an attorney. He's sharp and smart. He handles all the paperwork for the resort and everything, and fights fires on the side."

"Let him make Brad feel small," Tish said with a grin.

"Important question: are you in love with him?" Madison leaned forward, her gaze soft and understanding as she looked at me.

Emotion rushed through me, and I burst into tears. "Yes. And now I have to fix it." I sniffled.

"Okay, well, fix it," Luna said with an airy wave.

"I don't know what to do," I mumbled, feeling sheepish. Someone thrust a box of tissues in my direction, and I snagged a few to blow my nose and dab at my eyes.

"There is this thing called having a conversation. Crazy idea, I know," Chloe offered dryly.

A laugh sputtered out as I looked at her. "Wow."

"Just talk to him. Let him chase Brad away. You can hold your own," she said encouragingly.

"You already did," Madison pointed out. "You dumped Brad, right?"

I cleared my throat, nodding vigorously. "I did. Such a dick."

"When is the resort officially opening? Those Silver boys must be up to their eyeballs in work right now," Lucy chimed in.

"They are. It's crazy there," I said, my lips twisting to the side. "I'm going to talk to Haven as soon as I see him." I looked around at the women at the table. "Thank you."

"For what?" Amelia asked.

I felt bashful when I smiled. "For welcoming me here tonight. For, I guess, making me feel like I belong."

"Of course you belong," Amelia curled an arm around my shoulders and squeezed. "You're a badass. And we're glad you're back."

A little while later, as Chloe and I drove back toward the resort, she asked, "So what now?"

"I'm going to talk to Haven the first time I see him." My tone was resolute, even though I was a little nervous.

"Thank you," I said when she parked in front of the main resort at Heartfire Falls.

"For what?"

"For dragging me along with you tonight. I needed that."

Chloe's smile was warm. "Anytime."

We parted ways, and I tried to ignore the shaft of disappointment when I walked into the apartment upstairs in the barn and discovered Haven wasn't there.

I knew he would show up, so I planned to sit down and watch TV until he arrived. I needed something to distract me. Except I got paged from work. A whale was stranded in the mudflats off Turnagain Arm.

Chapter Thirty-Five

ELSA

I sped through the late evening dusk, grateful for the long summer evenings of Alaska. The fields of fireweed were ablaze as I drove past them.

The report was from some motorists who'd noticed a gray whale stranded near the mudflats. It sounded like we were lucky as far as location went. It was just north of where it would have been nearly impossible and unsafe for us to try to get out there and help. The mudflats were just what they sounded like and tricky to deal with because you could get stuck in the mud. There were signs all along them warning people from walking out. Fortunately, this whale was stranded in a sandy stretch of the shoreline. I parked along the side of the road and hurried out, buckets in hand, cell phone tucked into my pocket.

Dealing with stranded whales was fairly straightforward. If they were going to survive, you needed to keep them wet until the tide came in and try to help them get upright if needed. My boss was out of town, and I knew I would need help if the tide didn't come in soon. Fortunately, the whale was upright and clear of any boulders. While I was on my own, I draped wet sheets on the whale and focused on pouring water over it, careful to stay clear of the blowhole. When I got the call from the wildlife hotline, they confirmed they would notify the closest state troopers to assist, so I was counting on help arriving soon. Although the troopers covered large geographical areas in Alaska, so I had no idea when they might arrive.

"Honey, we are going to get you and your baby reunited. You're going to make it," I told her encouragingly. Maybe she didn't understand my words, but I hoped she understood my intent. I could feel her distress. Her calf was lingering in the deeper water in the inlet along with the rest of her pod.

Darkness began to fall, and I was starting to despair that help wasn't coming. I'd expected the troopers to arrive by now. The reception was spotty, but I fished my phone out of my pocket between pouring buckets of water on the whale.

Knowing I needed more people, I texted Haven.

Me: *I'm off the side of the highway in Turnagain Arm, just north of the mudflats. There's a whale stranded. The tide isn't going to be in for a few more hours, and we need help and we need lights.*

I tapped send before adding another text.

Me: *I love you. I'm sorry I got upset.*

Chapter Thirty-Six

HAVEN

I was pacing in the apartment above the barn when I got the text from Elsa.

I grabbed my fishing waders and an extra pair for Elsa in case she didn't bring hers, along with a change of clothes in case she was wet. After that, I jogged over to the main lodge, hoping to find my brothers.

"What's up?" Jude and Cole were lounging on the couch in front of the TV.

"Keep it down. I don't want Tommy to hear us," I said. "We need to go."

"Where?" Cole asked, just as Asher came walking into the room.

"I just got a text from Elsa. She's dealing with a stranded whale. The tide won't be in for a few hours. She says she's just north of the mudflats, so we need to get down there."

Not for the first time, I thanked the stars for my brothers. They didn't even hesitate to jump into action, with Asher racing to find Grady to come along as well.

We took two trucks and drove through the falling darkness.

"Do you know where she is?" Jude asked from my side. He was with me while Cole, Asher, and Grady were in Cole's truck. We'd left

Tommy home with our mom. Close enough to his bedtime, I'd known it wouldn't be a good plan to bring him along.

"We should see her car. Cell reception isn't great there, and I don't want to drain her battery by calling until we find her."

"Good point. We'll find her."

I added some pressure to the gas pedal.

"You okay?" he asked after silence stretched for a few moments.

"As okay as I can be."

"You don't seem all that okay," Jude pointed out. His tone wasn't even a little teasing.

"I might be freaking out," I admitted. "I'm not going to be okay until I know Elsa's okay."

"You love her." His words fell between us, quiet and low.

My heart felt lodged in my throat. "I do. She's pissed at me because I told that Brad guy to stay the fuck away from her."

"Ah, I see. Well, he's an ass," Jude offered dryly.

I chuckled. "He *is* an ass."

Blessedly, Jude dropped any conversation about my feelings after that, thank fuck. I knew maybe I'd overstepped when it came to Brad, and I was still stewing a little, knowing part of what I'd done was fueled by jealousy. I knew Elsa could protect herself, but for fuck's sake, I wanted to drive my fist into that guy's face.

Instead, I'd have to make do with making sure he couldn't fuck with Elsa.

It was close to dark by the time we saw Elsa's car. Of course, dark in late summer in Alaska was after ten o'clock. Cole parked behind us, and we all tumbled out.

On our way out, we'd grabbed as many lights as we could from the resort—construction lights and large battery-powered flashlights.

"Elsa!" I called.

I was relieved when I heard her voice in return. "Over here!"

We swung the lights around until we saw her standing in the water with a whale and a bucket.

"We called the troopers, right?" Cole asked, his tone dry.

"I already did," I replied. "They're headed this way too. We might be here for a few hours."

"We should ask them to bring takeout," Grady piped up.

I chuckled, slightly relieved for the humor because my worry was spinning tight inside. I grabbed the wading gear for Elsa after I pulled on my own. She was soaked and shivering as she stood beside the whale.

"Elsa, we need to get you dry," I said when I reached her side.

"I know. I was in a rush to leave and forgot to get my waders." Her worried gaze met mine, and my heart twisted.

"You go get dry and change," Jude ordered her. "We'll keep pouring water on this whale. We can stay here all night if needed."

"Troopers are headed down here too," I added.

Elsa let out a breath, stroking her hand over the massive whale. "I thought they'd be here by now."

"Whoever reported this just called the wildlife hotline, and they notified the troopers, but the message sat in voice mail," Asher explained as we walked back to the truck. "That's what the troopers said when I called."

Elsa was shivering. "Sweetheart, why didn't you call me sooner?" I asked.

"I was in a hurry and thought the troopers would be here." Her breath slipped out. "And you weren't home, and I yelled at you the last time I saw you." She blinked, giving her head a quick shake.

"Let's get you dry and changed."

"I'm not leaving," she replied, her words edged with stubbornness.

"I know you're not leaving," I returned. "We're gonna get this whale through the night, and hopefully, the tide rises enough soon."

"It's already coming in. I can hear the rest of them waiting for her," Elsa said.

"I know. She's got friends, just like you do."

"I'm worried her calf is stressed," she fretted.

"Probably."

While I nudged her away to my truck, Elsa continued rambling with worry about the whale, and all the while, my heart felt split wide open. Elsa loved wildlife as much as she loved humans.

By the time she dried off and changed, I was relieved she wasn't shivering anymore. She didn't even want to bother eating when the troopers arrived, having actually done as Asher had requested and brought takeout from a nearby gas station that served pizza.

"We're here to help and set up as many lights as you need," one of the troopers called out.

"Thank you. We love you!" Elsa called through the gloaming, with the lights shining on the whale as we poured water over it.

I didn't even know how long we were out there until the tide rose. Between us and two of the troopers, once we had enough water underneath the whale to get her pushed off the sand, Elsa cheered and burst into tears as the whale swam into the deeper water on her own.

We were all overcome with emotion. She jumped up and down and threw her arms around me. "Thank you!"

She proceeded to hug everybody there. Standing in the water as the lights shone out over it, we watched the pod of whales circling the mama whale, and the calf sidled up to her. It was kind of hard to tell in the darkness, but I could have sworn they were thanking us when they collectively blew misty air and water from their spouts.

We were all salty and sandy as we climbed back into our trucks.

Standing by the passenger door by Elsa's car, Jude looked from me to Elsa. "Want me to drive your car back?" he asked.

"Oh!" Elsa gave her head a little shake. "I forgot to consider that. If you don't mind, that would be great."

Jude flashed a quick grin. "I offered." After she fished her keys out, he hopped in and waved.

I waited for a moment after Elsa was in the truck. Relief gusted through me. The whales were safe, and she was safe. I turned to face her. Words were boomeranging around as I struggled to collect my thoughts.

"Elsa," I finally said, my voice hoarse with emotion rushing through me. "I wanted to talk to you tonight."

Her eyes were big in the dim glow of the dashboard lights.

I took an unsteady breath, turning to face her and reaching over to palm her cheek. "Are you okay?"

She blinked. "Yes."

Her hand curled on my wrist, sliding up and down as if to comfort me. Touching her after a few nights of not touching her was like throwing a lit match into dry kindling.

"I missed you," I murmured as I leaned across the console and pressed a kiss to her forehead. When I lifted my head, she tugged me back and brought her mouth to mine.

I poured so much feeling into that kiss. It was messy and open and hot. It was so much more need than lust. *Love* didn't even capture how much she meant to me.

"I didn't mean to scare you." She blinked, her lips swollen from our kiss. "Our office is the first place they call when there are stranded whales, and my boss is out of town, and some—"

I shook my head. "You don't need to explain. I just missed you, and when I couldn't get ahold of you and saw your text..." I gestured toward the dark ocean inlet. "I was a little worried."

"I know, but the whale's fine, her calf is fine, and everybody's safe."

I cleared my throat. "Next time, can you text me before you drive out into the darkness?"

She smiled sheepishly. "I will. I wasn't thinking. It's been... Well, should we drive home now?" she asked softly.

"Yes." With my emotions spinning inside, I needed something to focus on and slow my thoughts down.

"We can talk on the way," she said with a little laugh when I leaned close to give her another kiss.

"We can." I was reluctant to even drop my hand away from her, but there was only one way to drive. Driving wasn't going to work with me leaning across the console and kissing her over and over again.

Once I started driving, with the beam of lights on the road ahead of us as we wound through the turn upon turn of Turnagain Arm, I spoke, "I know I overstepped by interfering with Brad. I just—"

"It's okay. I overreacted. I could have handled it myself, but I appreciate what you were doing. Brad is a jerk, and he can be pushy. And to be honest, him hearing it from you and knowing that you could be a real nuisance to him is probably best."

"I know you can handle it yourself," I replied gruffly. I reached over, squeezing her knee.

When I turned my hand over, she laced her fingers in mine. Just being able to touch her soothed the rampage of emotions and desire coursing through me.

"Sometimes I can be overprotective," I said with a chuckle.

She squeezed my hand, and I was relieved when she giggled. "As long as you understand that I can take care of myself."

"Sweetheart, I *know* you can take care of yourself."

I took a breath, feeling the tension bundled inside me ease slightly. "How long were you with Brad?"

"You don't need to worry about Brad at all," she said quickly.

"I know that. I'm just curious."

"Are you jealous?" When I slid my gaze to hers, her eyes were wide with disbelief.

I bit my lip, wanting to fib, but this was Elsa. This was us. "Maybe a smidge. Don't worry. It wasn't like I thought you still had a thing for the guy, but I was like, *what the fuck? Who is this guy?*"

Elsa sighed, the sound deep and heartfelt. "I haven't had the best judgment in men. Present company excluded."

"Oh, so I'm a good choice?" I teased lightly, trying to ignore the doubts that so often clamored in my mind. Not specifically about Elsa, but about whether I could be everything she needed and deserved.

"Definitely." She twisted her lips with an eye roll before shaking her head. "You knew my childhood, Haven. I just... I never felt like I fit in. And that's saying something when you're from Alaska, you know?"

"I know. I get it."

"My dad let my mom down a lot, even though he loved her. My therapist said I might have some issues with feeling emotionally abandoned because of how he died, and that he could've tried to help himself, but he didn't. She said that sometimes that plays out in feeling like you might *literally* be abandoned. Unconsciously, I found men who weren't like my dad at all. Like, had their life together. All the traditional trappings, financial success, regular job, all that." Elsa circled her hand in the air. "And quirky guys like my dad are a better fit for me. I guess? But you're not like my dad either."

I chuckled. "Uh, no, I don't think so."

"When you stepped in with Brad, all my reactions kicked in, so I panicked." She paused. "I hate admitting the next part."

Haven stroked his thumb over the back of my hand and down along the edge of my wrist. His touch was soothing yet also distracting. But then, Haven distracted me all the time.

"What do you hate admitting, sweet Elsa?" His low voice spun around my heart.

"I just feel so stupid. I wanted an asshole like Brad to like me. When he showed up at Heartfire Falls, all I could think was what an idiot I'd been. It's not just him. He's kind of the pinnacle of me being a foolish girl, trying to impress people who aren't worth my time. He pushed every button on my insecurity." I cleared my throat, feeling that familiar sense of shame.

"Sweetheart, we all make mistakes."

"Did you ever date somebody who treated you like that?"

Haven's gaze slid to mine. "Not specifically somebody like Brad, but life's life. I've done dumb shit."

I eyed him skeptically. "I know better now, but more than once, I believed my heart was broken by guys who weren't even worth a shred of my time and energy. I just feel so stupid. Brad was so confident he could take advantage of me again."

Haven squeezed my hand. "Elsa, you figured it out when you were ready to figure it out. You *weren't* stupid. One of the things I love about you is that you really wear your heart on your sleeve. I know that's kind of a cliché, but you do. You're kind to everybody. You give everybody a chance. Maybe sometimes that means you've given people a chance who didn't deserve it. But..." Haven let out a weary-sounding sigh. "I'm the cynical asshole who assumes the worst of too many people."

I squeezed his hand now. "No, you're not."

His gaze flicked to mine as he rolled his eyes briefly before shifting his attention back to the road. "See, you're going to try to be nice about it. But even before our dad died, before the fire, and before Bree died, I was never that guy who was going to give everybody an easy chance."

My heart flipped over in my chest. "Maybe not, and maybe I am too trusting. I appreciate that you're trying to put a good spin on me being foolish." I let out a little laugh. "But I *did* figure it out. Of course, I thought I was being all slick with you."

"Slick? What do you mean?"

"As if I could do this thing where I would keep it casual." I paused because everything felt like *a lot*. "I've been half in love with you since the first time we kissed."

"Well, I told you I had a crush on you in high school."

He couldn't see me, but I rolled my eyes. "Maybe so, but it was just high school," I insisted.

"When we had the argument, you said that thing about me keeping my distance and how you understood what that meant. I know I do that, and I know it's not helpful," he said. "Also, just ask my brothers."

"Ask your brothers *what*?" I pressed.

"How big my crush was on you."

"Oh, my God," I mumbled, my cheeks heating in the darkness.

He shook his head. "The truth is you were my high school fantasy."

"What?!" I yelped.

"All the way. You were the girl next door, and you were so cute and funny. You were always nice. Meanwhile, I was the big, awkward guy." He shook his head with a wondering sigh. "So yeah, you were."

I gaped at him. He flicked me a glance, then returned his attention to the road.

"Now you know the whole truth, nothing but the truth, so help me God," he teased.

"Wow," I breathed, trying to absorb this.

For the first time, I sensed just how honest Haven was being. "Look, you're *that* girl for me. You always have been, and I need to be clear about something. It's not like I was angling when you needed a place to stay. I figured I'd have to keep my shit together, but I also thought that old crush was nothing much. I was wrong on that count."

I squeezed his hand. "Wow. My life would have turned out so much better if I'd known you had a crush on me back then."

Haven shook his head. "I think our timing is better now. We were young, and you moved away."

"I know, but—"

"Elsa, our time is now. We get to keep all the good things."

"Thank you," he said a moment later after quiet had stretched between us.

"For what?"

"For giving me a little more understanding about what was behind all your feelings around Brad."

"What? I don't have feelings around Brad."

Haven circled his hand in the air. "The situation. You know what I mean."

"Oh, okay. By the way, that's all resolved. Between you and Janet's lawyer friend, Brad backed off. Not like he had anything other to do other than try to bullshit me, but I haven't heard a peep from him since. By the way, thank you."

"For what?" he teased.

"For telling me you had a crush on me in high school. You were the older guy then."

His chuckle vibrated through my body. "I guess I was, huh?"

"You guess? It's plain math."

When he snorted, I started laughing, and then we both were. By the time it petered out, I was breathless. I *needed* that laugh. "Thanks for coming to help with the whale."

"Anytime you need help with a stranded whale, I'm your guy," he said matter-of-factly.

My throat felt tight with emotion. "I know you are."

"I'm not going anywhere. You know that, right?"

"I know. You're stuck with me."

"I'll keep you," he teased.

We fell quiet as he drove through the darkness with a few pauses for moose crossing the road. Just as we turned onto the drive that led to Heartfire Falls, the lights from his truck illuminated a cluster of animals ahead.

My mouth dropped open. "It's a pack of wolves!" I whisper-shouted.

Haven's teeth flashed with his smile. "It is. We don't see them much. I know they're around, but they lay low."

We watched as the pack ambled across the driveway. I counted eleven. "My dad used to say there were wolf packs around, but I never saw them," I said. "Usually, I heard coyotes calling at night."

"They're clearly comfortable here," Haven said as he swung his hand across the dash.

They weren't in any hurry and didn't seem bothered by the truck's lights illuminating their way into the trees.

When we walked into the apartment a few minutes later, Haven kissed me, and I tumbled into it. Things heated as fast as a flame racing through dry grass. I almost lost my balance, and we broke apart, gasping.

"Shower," Haven said.

I didn't need further instruction. He kicked the door shut behind us. Our clothes were tossed in a tangle as we made our way across the room, stumbling into the bathroom. We showered together with messy kisses before we made our way into what I now thought of as *our* room. Haven bent me over the bed, and I sighed when his fingers delved between my thighs.

"Oh, sweetheart, I missed you so fucking much," he rasped.

I savored the feel of the hot kisses he dropped down my spine. "Hurry." I was so impatient.

I let out a sigh of relief when I felt the thick press of his crown at my entrance and the delicious stretch when he filled me in one deep thrust. I was desperate and needy. Everything was a rush when he reached around, teasing his fingers over my swollen bud.

My climax was a fiery burst exploding through me, his name the only word I could say as I trembled. I cried out when he withdrew. He turned me around and eased me over the bed, murmuring, "I need to see you."

When he filled me again, my climax felt as if it never ended. One rolled into the next as he rocked into me deeply, his eyes holding mine. One hand cupped my cheek, and the other laced with mine as we clung to each other in the storm that spun around us.

That intimacy felt like a net of sparks and love holding us together. "I love you," he whispered before bringing one hand between us to tip me over the edge once again. As I shuddered against him, I savored the heat of his release filling me, whispering through broken breaths, "Love you..."

Chapter Thirty-Eight

HAVEN

Sunshine woke me the following morning. The light was angling through the windows because, for obvious reasons, we hadn't thought to close the curtains the night before. When I rolled my head on the pillows, I discovered Elsa curled on her side, the sun catching on the glints of gold in her hair.

My lips curled into a smile. We were tangled up together. Oh, how I'd missed this.

Maybe it had only been a matter of days, but those days had been long and the nights even longer. I couldn't resist sifting my fingers through her hair, watching the way the sunlight flickered like strands of gold with the motion.

I slid my hand down her back. Her skin was warm, and of course, my palm slid right over the sweet curve of her bottom because I couldn't help it. Her lips curved into a smile, and her eyes opened to meet mine.

"Hey," she murmured, her voice softened on the edges from sleep, a little raspy.

"Hey."

I had to clear my throat, and suddenly, my heart felt tight because everything felt real. Not that it hadn't been before, but we'd put voice to so much last night.

"I know where we should go," I said, surprising myself with even the thought.

"Where?"

"To Spruce Green."

Her eyes widened slightly before she nodded. "We should. Let's go before breakfast."

We tumbled out of bed and into the shower. Of course, by the time we were out and getting dressed, my knees were a little weak.

Starting the day with Elsa was everything I wanted. I hoped I could look forward to thousands more mornings with her.

Our breath misted in the air as we walked to my truck. The distant bleating of a goat elicited a chuckle. A short drive later, we walked hand in hand in the cemetery. We stopped first in front of Bree's marker.

"I miss her," I said softly.

Elsa squeezed my hand. "I know you do."

My throat ached with it when the grief slammed into me for a moment. Even though years had passed since my sister died, my grief still hovered. At first, you tricked yourself into thinking the worst had passed, but then you learned that some days, the weight of it was almost paralyzing. On other days, there was a sharpness to it, like a blade slicing through your heart just to remind you.

I cleared my throat, lifting Elsa's hand to brush a kiss on the back of it. "But we'll be open soon, and I know she'd love what we've done at Heartfire Falls."

Elsa's laugh was soft. "I'm sure of it."

"Where's your dad's grave?"

Elsa and I walked just a few steps before she traced her fingertips over her father's name.

"We cremated him too, in case that wasn't obvious." She took a big breath, letting it out in a gust. "My dad was such a funny guy."

"He always seemed like it," I offered.

"I was surprised when he died. My mom wasn't, but I was because I didn't really understand." She wrinkled her nose. "Once I understood,

I was angry for a while. I'm not anymore, but it didn't have to happen, you know?"

"I know."

Last, we walked back to my dad's marker, just above Bree's.

"You miss him," Elsa said softly, squeezing my hand.

"Always." My voice was hushed.

We walked out, following the stone path, our hands laced, the wind gusting and the fireweed swaying in the distance. It felt fitting that we did this together. While the details were different, loss left scars, and we needed to acknowledge them.

As we drove back to Heartfire Falls, I asked, "When is your mom coming to visit?"

"She hasn't confirmed a time yet." Elsa let out a soft breath. "I'm just happy she might come at all."

I glanced her way briefly. "I know you are." An easy quiet fell between us as I drove, until we got close to home. I smiled when my eyes landed on the sign Elsa had painted for us. "That sign is beautiful. Thank you again."

"I did it for you all," she said softly. "I'm glad you like it."

"You did it for *us*," I corrected.

Her eyes met mine when I parked the truck.

"Us?"

"Sunshine, you're it for me. Us," I said softly.

I leaned over to give her a lingering kiss, breaking apart when we heard Tommy calling from the porch steps. "Breakfast!"

Moments later, I circled my hand between his shoulder blades as we walked through the doors. "What'd you make today?"

"Pancakes and bacon."

"Grandma let you make some bacon?" I asked.

His head bobbed. "Yeah. Although I had to be all careful, and she made me put this screen thing over the pan, and I didn't like cleaning it."

Elsa giggled. "Smart move. Bacon grease is no joke when it's hot."

A few minutes later, I looked over at Elsa, who ended up across the table from me as she declared Tommy's pancakes and bacon the best she'd ever had. My heart kicked hard and fast.

EPILOGUE

Kendall Castille

"Oh no. Travis!" I hissed.

My husky looked up at me, blinking with innocence in his blue eyes. I knew better. When I turned to look at the dress I was supposed to wear to the wedding, his gaze followed mine. Not my wedding, mind you, but it started in an hour, and the dress I was supposed to wear was perfect for my three-legged husky to rub his whole muddy body all over.

He sidled against my legs, giving an affectionate snort. "You don't even care, do you?" I glanced down at him.

His tail wagged before he let out a nice little roo for me. "Oh my God," I muttered.

When my phone rang, I didn't glance at the screen before answering it. "What?"

"Well, hello to you too. Sounds like you're having a great morning," Jude Silver teased. "I'm on my way to pick you up."

"I know," I ground out, "but I have a small problem."

"What's that?"

"Travis got muddy this morning, and, well, now the mud that was on his fur is all over the dress I was supposed to wear."

Jude didn't even try not to laugh, letting out a deep, hearty *bark* of a laugh. "No need to stress. It'll be fine."

"Jude," I protested. "It's a wedding. Your *brother's* wedding. I care about Elsa and Haven, and I don't want to show up in a muddy dress for their wedding. I don't know what to wear, and I don't know what to do!" I threw my hands up in the air as I paced.

Travis was now worried about me. Not because of the dress, mind you, but he sensed my stress, so he danced along at my side, tippy-tapping his feet on the floor.

"You have another dress or something, right?"

"Jude," I ground out, "I'm not exactly a dress girl."

I ignored the way his chuckle played over the edges of my nerves in an unsettling way.

"Not exactly. Well, I'm still coming to get you." He paused. "You could always go to the wedding naked." Electric pause this time. "Okay, maybe that came out the wrong way."

I sighed. "Maybe it did, Jude. I'll figure it out. What's your ETA?"

"Ten minutes."

"Ten minutes?!" I yelped.

"See you in a few," he replied with a chuckle.

The line clicked, and I threw my phone on my bed. Racing around my room, I frantically looked for *anything* to wear. Finally settling on a skirt and a blouse, I glared down at my dog.

"This is not exactly wedding-worthy, but it'll have to do. I wish *you* had to get dressed for a wedding." Travis's tail just wagged along.

I hustled to get dressed and refused to even look at the clock. I didn't need to waste time counting the seconds. Small problem with that, though.

My apartment was a studio, just one big space with the living room and kitchen all together and the bed tucked in a little alcove. Everything was visible when you came through the door. Except the bathroom, which did have a door. But my closet? It was also out in the main area.

Maybe I was overexplaining. I was prone to doing that, but you need to have a sense of the context for what happened next.

Jude was my best friend. We'd become close in middle school, and that never changed. We had keys to each other's places. He could just walk in. That was the kind of thing that would be okay—except for *now*.

In my haste, compounded by my choice not to obsess over the time, just as I was adjusting my skirt—one of those wrap skirts that needed to be tied just so—there was a sharp knock on the door. Before I could say a word, the door swung open, and Jude stepped inside.

There I stood with my skirt halfway tied with no shirt, no bra, nothing up top. My breasts were fully on display. My eyes whipped up to collide with Jude's. His big, beautiful blues went wide, and I could have sworn he actually stopped breathing for a few seconds.

I felt the blush bloom all over my skin, the heat starting on my chest, rising up my neck and into my cheeks. I tried to breathe, but I was frozen, my hands still holding the stupid wrap skirt. As we stared at each other, my nipples—*my freaking nipples*—tightened like they were happy to see him.

Fire spun in my belly, sending sparks scattering through me. I took the moment to absorb him. Jude's black hair was damp. His blue eyes were bright with flashes of silver. Sweet hell, he was so freaking handsome. Tall, broad shoulders, lean, and unfairly fit. The man's lifestyle demanded that kind of fitness. He was a wilderness guide, an outdoor survival expert, a first responder, and a hotshot firefighter. He was manliness wrapped in lumberjack and topped off with a dose of too sexy for his own good. And apparently, for my nipples.

He wore a royal blue shirt over slacks. He looked much tamer than usual. The man practically lived in battered jeans and T-shirts, all of which did nothing other than show off his sexy, hot bod. But tucking this wild man into civilized clothing for a wedding somehow made him all the sexier.

My lungs abandoned any effort to get air, and my pulse had taken off so fast there was no catching it. We simply stood there and stared at each other for God knows how long until Jude snapped the moment.

"For fuck's sake, Kendall?" he burst out as he spun around. "Get dressed!" He clasped the back of his neck, his head bowed.

"I *am* getting dressed!" I protested.

"You knew I was arriving in ten minutes!"

"Yeah, and I just told you on the phone that Travis ruined my dress! Well, maybe not ruined, but for the purposes of today, I can't wear it!" I flung my arm toward the dress in question, which was draped over the back of the couch.

It was my own damn fault. My dog loved rubbing his back along the couch. It was like a personal scratching post for him.

"Get dressed," Jude ground out.

JUDE

Roughly an hour after picking Kendall up for the wedding, I looked ahead at my eldest brother, who had just said his part of the vows.

Haven was oblivious to everything but Elsa. His eyes were locked on her as she stood in front of him. They were getting married outside, and it was a beautiful day for an outdoor wedding. A soft breeze rustled through the air. The fireweed was in full bloom in the field nearby. All in all, there might as well have been birds chirping. Who knew my grumpy oldest brother could fall so hard that he would actually *not* be so cranky?

I took a breath, shifting my shoulders. "Are you okay?" Kendall whispered from where she sat beside me in the front row of chairs.

"Fine," I all but hissed through my teeth.

"Sheesh, I was just asking," she muttered.

After this afternoon, I would never, *ever*, *ever* walk into any space again after knocking without waiting for someone to tell me to come in. Walking in and seeing Kendall bare from the waist up had nearly undone me. I was still trying to recover. And honestly? I didn't know if I ever *would* recover.

We'd been friends since middle school when she moved to town. For years, I'd tried to pretend that I didn't have that big of a crush on her in high school. Except I knew better. But then, I'd convinced myself I'd gotten over it.

For a few years, we'd both gone our separate ways. Kendall left town for college. And well, my life, along with the rest of my family's, had been a hot mess for the past decade or so.

So it had been fine. No crushes for me. Then she moved back, and we fell back into our friendship. It was *all* fine.

But, as of roughly an hour ago, I knew what her breasts looked like, and they were perfect. Absolutely perfect. But then, *she* was perfect. With her wild brown curls, her big blue eyes, the freckles on her cheeks, her cute little body, curvy and soft-looking. Now, I was forever cursed with the knowledge that her breasts were more than a handful and her nipples were a light, dusky pink and puckered up beautifully. So beautifully that it had been *all* I could do not to walk across that room in her apartment, cup both breasts in my hands, and suck her perky nipples into my mouth.

I was going to fantasize about that, well, probably for the rest of my fucking life. It would be torture. Her perfect nipples were the problem.

Well, her nipples weren't the problem. The problem was I was half in love with her, and she was my best friend, and I didn't want to screw up our friendship. Yet now my mind would be forever filled with the images of her breasts and the way her skin flushed.

Fuck me.

Kendall's breath drew in with a soft sound of surprise, and I glanced over to see tears shining in her eyes as she pressed her palm against her chest.

Oh, that's right. We were at a wedding, and my eldest brother was pledging himself to the woman he loved. *Focus, focus, focus.*

I brought my attention back to the happy couple. They must have just been pronounced man and wife because Haven dipped his head to kiss Elsa.

The next few hours were a blur. No matter how hard I tried *not* to pay attention to Kendall, it was impossible. She was like a magnet for me. I might as well have been physically attached to her. Of course, we were good friends, and we truly were, so everyone kind of expected us to hang out together because we usually did. Spending time with Kendall was usually one of my favorite things. *Until I saw her breasts today.*

"Congratulations, man." I clapped Haven on the shoulder and pulled him into a back-slapping hug.

He chuckled. "I'm finally married," he said, looking almost surprised.

"You are. Elsa is perfect for you," I said, meaning it in a way that I couldn't have imagined, even at the beginning of their relationship.

"She is. Thank you."

"For what?" I prompted.

"Being my brother. Being here. Giving me a nudge when I needed to get my head straight. About Elsa, all that stuff," Haven explained.

"Anytime, man. That's what brothers are for, right?"

"Something like that," Asher, another brother, said dryly from my side.

I chuckled, sliding my eyes to him.

"It's your turn," Asher announced.

"Excuse me?"

"I'm just kidding, but now that Haven's fallen, somebody else has to."

"Well, it's *not* gonna be me," I said flatly.

"Oh, I think you're the most obvious one," Asher returned.

"Why?" I was flummoxed.

He narrowed his eyes, his expression knowing as he glanced over toward Kendall.

Her makeshift wedding outfit looked amazing on her. It was a wrap skirt with a silky blouse on top. Of course, all I could do was picture her without the blouse. I wanted to lift her hips onto a counter, drape that skirt around her thighs, and—

Well, there went my thoughts again. Slow your roll, dude.

"You're in love with Kendall," Asher said flatly.

"What?!" I exclaimed.

Haven overheard and chuckled. "Maybe you haven't figured it out, but the rest of us have," he pointed out. "Anytime you want to talk about it, I'm here. After our honeymoon."

Elsa appeared at his side after parting with her mother who angled over to chat with ours. "What's happening after our honeymoon?" she asked.

Haven grinned. "Jude is in love with Kendall, and I told him we all know it, even if *he* doesn't."

Elsa nodded, her gaze understanding as she glanced at me. "When you're ready, Jude, you can face it."

"Oh my God," I muttered.

Of course, the part that killed me the most about this entire ridiculous conversation was the one person I wanted to vent to was Kendall.

"Wow." I looked among them. "How about you guys steer clear of the gossip? Not cool."

"You're family," Elsa said matter-of-factly.

"It's not gossip, just observation," Haven added, his gaze teasing.

"All right, lovebirds. Off with you. It's getting late," I finally said. "Do you need a ride to the airport tomorrow?"

"Actually, that'd be awesome." They were flying to Hawaii for their honeymoon. Elsa insisted she needed somewhere tropical.

"You got it," I replied, relieved they let me drop the burning-hot topic of Kendall.

When the happy couple moved along, Asher glanced over, one brow rising. "Looking for Kendall, aren't you?"

"Oh, shut the fuck up. I'm giving her a ride home."

Asher chuckled, but then his gaze sobered. "I won't tease you." He paused. "I mean, just a little." He held up his thumb and forefinger with a tiny space between them.

"Fuck you," I teased before turning and threading my way through the crowd to find Kendall.

The space inside my truck was unusually quiet as I drove her home. I contemplated whether I should discuss what happened. Then, like an idiot, I started the conversation. "So should we talk about that, or..."

"No, we shouldn't talk about that. In fact, why don't you just forget what you saw?"

I almost choked. "Well, that's impossible, Kendall."

When I glanced her way as I parked my truck, her eyes were wide. "Why is it impossible?"

"Because you're fucking beautiful, Kendall. And now I know you have perfect breasts," I said flatly.

. . .

Thank you for reading Elsa & Haven's story! Want a glimpse of the future for them? Join my newsletter to receive an exclusive scene.

Sign up here: https://BookHip.com/VQXVKGT

p.s. If you are already subscribed, you'll still be able to access the scene.

Up next is in Heartfire Falls is Mine To Hold.

Best friends don't kiss… unless they're ready to break every rule.

I've been half in love with Kendall forever, all the while hiding it behind our friendship. Now the spark between us burns too hot to ignore, and crossing that line might just change everything.

One-click: Mine To Hold due out early 2026!

For more swoon & sass…

This Crazy Love kicks off the Swoon Series - small town southern romance with enough heat to melt you! Jackson & Shay's story is epic - swoon-worthy & intensely emotional. Jackson just happens to be Shay's brother's best friend. He's also *seriously* easy on the eyes. Shay has a past, the kind of past she would most definitely like to forget. Past or not, Jackson is about to rock her world. Don't miss their story!

Burn For Me is a second chance romance for the ages. Sexy firefighters? Check. Rugged men? Check. Wrapped up together? Check. Brave the fire in this hot, small-town romance. Amelia & Cade were high school sweethearts & then it all fell apart. When they cross paths again, it's epic - don't miss Cade's story!

For more small town romance, take a visit to Last Frontier Lodge in

Diamond Creek. A sexy, alpha SEAL meets his match with a brainy heroine in Take Me Home. Marley is all brains & Gage is all brawn. Sparks fly when their worlds collide. Don't miss Gage & Marley's story!

If sports romance lights your spark, check out The Play. Liam is a British footballer who falls for Olivia, his doctor. A twist of forbidden heats up this swoon-worthy & laugh-out-loud romance. Don't miss Liam & Olivia's story.

Be sure to sign up for my newsletter for the latest news, teasers & more! Click here to sign up: http://jhcroixauthor.com/subscribe/

FIND MY BOOKS

Thank you for reading What We Keep! I hope you enjoyed the story. If so, you can help other readers find my books in a variety of ways.

1) Write a review!
2) Sign up for my newsletter, so you can receive information about upcoming new releases & receive a FREE copy of one of my books: http://jhcroixauthor.com/subscribe/
3) Like and follow my Amazon Author page at https://amazon.com/author/jhcroix
4) Follow me on Bookbub at https://www.bookbub.com/authors/j-h-croix
5) Follow me on Instagram at https://www.instagram.com/jhcroix/
6) Like my Facebook page at https://www.facebook.com/jhcroix

Heartfire Falls Series
What We Keep

Mine To Hold - coming 2026!

Wild Fire Series
All The Afters
When We Dare
Fake It True
Only Ever You
Just For Us - coming 2026!
Fireweed Harbor Series
Make You Mine
Dare To Fall
Be The One
One More Time
Wait For You
Ever After All
Light My Fire Series
Wild With You
Hold Me Now
Only Ever Us
Fall For Me
Keep Me Close
With Every Breath
All It Takes
Take Me Now
Meant To Be
Dare With Me Series
Crash Into You
Evers & Afters
Come To Me
Back To Us
Take Me There
After We Fall
Swoon Series
This Crazy Love
Wait For Me

Break My Fall
Truly Madly Mine
Still Go Crazy
If We Dare
Steal My Heart
Into The Fire Series
Burn For Me
Slow Burn
Burn So Bad
Hot Mess
Burn So Good
Sweet Fire
Play With Fire
Melt With You
Burn For You
Crash & Burn
That Snowy Night
Haven's Bay Holiday Series
All I Want
All I Need
All We Have
All We Are
Brit Boys Sports Romance
The Play
Big Win
Out Of Bounds
Play Me
Naughty Wish
Diamond Creek Alaska Novels
When Love Comes
Follow Love
Love Unbroken
Love Untamed
Tumble Into Love
Christmas Nights
Lodge Series

ACKNOWLEDGMENTS

Thank you, thank you, thank you - to every reader who takes a chance on my stories. New and old, near and far. I remain profoundly grateful to all of you.

Many thanks to my editor for helping me shape the story, to Terri D. for patiently proofreading after multiple other rounds of editing and reminding me yet again that there are things like time and days of the week. Thank you to my early readers who let me know about any lingering mistakes.

Najla Qamber crafted a stunning design for this series. Erin is my assistant who catches the details I forget and works in the background to help me stay sane.

This book was plotted in my brain with a new dog to join our other one, and she's a sweet and sassy girl to go with our goofy boy. To DBC for supporting me through so many years and so many books.

xoxo

J.H. Croix

9 781965 224199